FIRST LOVE
NEVER
DIES

RONALD HANSEN

Goldewyn/United States

Goldewyn 227 Sandy Springs Place Suite D-404 Sandy Springs, GA 30328

ISBN:

978-1-64877-072-2 (paperback)

978-1-64877-073-9 (digital)

Library of Congress Cataloging-in-Publication

Library of Congress Control Number 2024935731

This book is entirely fictional. The names, characters, settings, and events depicted are either products of the author's creativity or are utilized in a fictitious manner. Any similarity to real-life events, places, or individuals, whether alive or deceased, is purely accidental.

Chapter One

The early morning sunlight filtered through the thin curtains as Meilan walked down the hallway of her childhood home. Though she had moved out on her own years ago, there were memories that haunted her, memories that she knew were still in this home. Meilan looked at the faded wallpaper that had been put up to cover the chipped paint beneath it. Some things never changed.

The dark-haired woman entered her old room. She allowed her gaze to drift over the pink sheets on the small bed that matched the gossamer drapes delicately billowing around the open window. Her parents had kept the bedroom exactly the same even after Meilan moved out. She sighed and ran a hand through her hair. It had been a while since she had returned to the room of her adolescent self. An uneasy feeling settled over her as she took in all of the pictures still hanging on the walls.

Approaching the framed photos on the wall, Meilan ran her fingers across the surface of one particular picture of a stern-faced man with gentle eyes the same pretty shade of gold as her own.

Three days had seemed to drag by since Meilan's father passed, and she still expected to hear his voice quietly echoing across the home. Her father was a brave man, and she liked to think she'd inherited that trait as well.

Years ago, Meilan's father made the decision to leave China, the only home he had ever known, and move his young family to the United States. It was there that her father knew he would be able to give them all a better life. At first, the culture shock was challenging. Meilan was barely able to speak a word of English when she started high school in New York City. She'd grown to adore the Big Apple, but just before her graduation, her father packed them up a second time to make the cross-country journey from New York to California.

Meilan didn't mind the warm and sunny beaches of California, but she couldn't help but feel that she'd left a part of her heart back in New York. That was, after all, where she'd met Jayden. Years had passed since they last spoke, but Meilan still thought of her old friend every single day.

Glancing over her shoulder, Meilan made sure that she was alone. Then, she bent down in front of her bookshelf to push aside a few carefully arranged texts. Hidden behind them was a small scrapbook that had been gifted to her shortly before she left New York. She sat down on the edge of her old bed and began tenderly flipping through the furled pages of the photo album. Some of the pictures had become discolored with age, the joyous smiles of the two best friends were still as vibrant as ever. Jayden had no idea when he gave Meilan this photo album that she was about to leave New York forever.

"Oh, Jay," she sighed softly, her fingers trailing over the contours of one picture. The glue was starting to come up, the photo slowly peeling away from the page. "Where are you right now?"

After her move to California, she'd written Jayden at least a hundred letters that he never responded to. She frowned and flipped the page, looking at another picture. Her stomach twisted. All of those letters had gone unanswered. To this day, she still felt as if she were to blame.

"What are you looking at?" someone asked from Meilan's doorway.

Meilan stiffened and looked up to see that her mother had wandered into the room. Her mother's eyes were still rimmed with red from the funeral of Meilan's father, but she brushed them away with the back of her quivering hand. There was nothing that her mother could do to hide the hollows under her eyes or the haunted look that lived there. Meilan looked over her mother, noting the thinness to her frame that hadn't been there before.

The death of her father was painful for the entire family but none more than her mother. Meilan used to envy the love that her parents had. Her parents had been together for years and though times weren't always easy, she had never seen a couple as in love as her parents. Even now, she wished to find a love that strong.

"It's an old scrapbook that Jay made me before we moved out here," said Meilan. Her parents had known how much Meilan's old friend meant to her, and now that she was grown up, there was no need to hide this photo album anymore. "I still can't believe he never answered any of my letters. Are you sure we had the right address?"

"Yes..." Meilan's mother answered after hesitating a moment.

Meilan bit her lip, lingering on a picture of Jayden for a moment before closing the little scrapbook. When she started school in New York, the other students had delighted in tormenting her. Maybe it was the way she spoke what little English she knew that bothered them. Perhaps they were just cruel and found joy in mocking others. She had never been interested in finding out. Though she didn't understand many of the insults her peers tossed her way, she knew they were insults. The other students treated her as an outcast, as if she wasn't worthy of walking their halls.

Not Jayden, never Jayden. At lunch every day, he would sit beside her and help her practice her English lessons. In the beginning, she hated the tattered notebook he used to bring with him. Not understanding all of the words that her classmates had grown up knowing was humiliating. He never laughed though. Not once. When she stumbled over a word or used the wrong one, he would help her understand the mistake. Meilan didn't think it had ever occurred to Jayden to treat her like the other students did.

It was after the second or third lunch period they shared that Meilan noticed Jayden never brought any food of his own. Whenever she pressed him about this, he would just laugh and say that he ate a big breakfast. However, one evening when Meilan had stayed late for extra tutoring, she saw him sneaking into the school's basement. The following confrontation was tough for both of them. The only person that had bothered to show her kindness was suffering. She knew that Jayden took no pleasure in swallowing his pride and telling her that he had been living in the school's basement for weeks. He told her about his foster home – too many children and not enough food to go around. Even when she had been standing there and talking to him, she could hear his stomach growling.

After that, Meilan began bringing two lunches. Whenever her mother asked why she needed two lunches, Meilan would tell her that she was hungry after gym class. Nobody else needed to know Jayden's secret, not even her mother. After a few weeks, her mother stopped questioning the extra food. Even if her mother wasn't working three jobs to make ends meet, she didn't have time to make lunch. Meilan took it upon herself to make the meals for both her and Jayden, thankful that her mother had taught her how to cook in China.

At first, Meilan was afraid that Jayden might make fun of the food that she brought. He had never made fun of her before but Americans were rarely excited about the things they didn't know. However, the first time that she placed the lunch box filled with bao in front of Jayden, she saw a single tear fall. He had been quick to wipe it away, pretending it had never happened though his eyes were still glossy as he ate.

"Are you that hungry, Jay?" Meilan had teased.

Jayden had looked at her with heartfelt sincerity brimming in his eyes and whispered, "This is the best food that I've ever tasted."

Even thinking about that moment now made Meilan's heart skip a beat. Looking back, she knew it was at that point that she started to fall for him. He was the boy living wherever he could make a bed for the night and she was a girl who just didn't belong among her peers. If they weren't destined to fall together, she would have been shocked.

As they grew older, Meilan set to work helping Jayden get his life together. Day and night they worked to find him a place to live and a job to pay the bills. Together they were able to bring stability to his life, food in his stomach, and a roof over his head.

Meilan had been more than happy to help her friend but she would be lying if she said that she hadn't been hoping that something more would occur. They were best friends, that was a given, but in all the books that she liked to read, the best friends always fell in love. Jayden was everything that Meilan wanted but the feeling never seemed to be reciprocated.

Why else had he ignored her letters?

Perhaps he was angry with her. Before she left the city, she hadn't been able to work up the courage to tell him that she was moving. It had been too much. Breaking both of their hearts would destroy her – of that much she was certain. Instead of telling her Jayden that she had to leave, she'd boarded the plane to California without as much as a goodbye to her best friend. She knew if she tried to look Jayden in his beautiful, dark eyes and say farewell, that she would have never stopped crying. She didn't want Jayden to remember her that way. Instead, she'd decided to write him letters, which she did. She had stayed up late night after night for weeks. Endless papers had littered her floor, remnants of the words that she tried to find but couldn't without him. What little she had been able to write felt as if her heart had been poured on the page.

Unfortunately, he'd never answered.

Her memories faded to the background; the love lost never quite leaving her mind. Meilan sighed and stood, tucking the scrapbook under her arm. It had been years and there was no use dwelling on the past anymore. If Jayden had wanted her in his life, he would have made an effort to do so. It wasn't until Meilan headed to the door that her mother spoke once more.

Growing up, Meilan had known that her mother was a quiet woman. Nothing had ever seemed to faze her. No matter what hardships her family went through, her mother was the rock. She stood silently behind both Meilan and her father, making sure that each of them achieved their dreams. As Meilan looked at her mother, she wondered for a moment if the older woman had ever achieved her dreams. Clearly, she had found love; that much was evident in the way her mother had always looked at both her and her father.

Meilan smiled, though she knew it didn't reach her eyes. How could it when she had lost the two most important men in her life? Her father had died and Jay had slipped through her fingers. She remembered the way her mother had held her as she cried, rocking her back and forth and bringing her tea as if it could sure all of the world's problems. For weeks, Meilan's mother had been the one to drag her out of bed and remind her of the dreams that Meilan had been working too hard to achieve. Without her mother, Meilan doubted that she would be where she was now.

"What is it, Mom? You don't look like you are feeling too well. Can I get you anything?"

Before her mother could answer, Meilan was turning around to set the scrapbook on the dresser, prepared to do whatever it took to help her mother. It couldn't be easy having the person you vowed to spend the rest of your life with pass away. Meilan would do everything that she could to make her mother comfortable and happy again. It was her duty as a daughter.

"I think there is something you should know, Meilan," her mother suddenly said. The tears in her mother's eyes began to streak down her cheeks. The older woman drew a shuddering breath and her voice grew strained as she spoke. "We didn't move just because your father got a new job as an herbalist in California. Now that your father is gone, I can be honest with you. We moved because he was afraid that your friendship with an African American boy would blossom into something more serious. Interracial relationships can be so hard and so full of stigma. We'd left China to live a better life, and he was worried about the struggles you might face if you fell in love with Jayden." Her mother's voice cracked. "Your father only had good intentions, Meilan, you have to believe that."

Why? Meilan thought. It was the first thing that came to her mind, hearing that their move so many years ago had been about not only her father's new job but leaving Jayden behind as well. Her father had been a good man; he always wanted what was best for his daughter. Now, it was hard for Meilan to hear such a hard truth, especially coming from her mother. Watching the tears fall from the older woman's eyes, Meilan knew that her mother was telling the truth.

Meilan's heart raced. She gripped the book close to her chest, tears welling in her eyes as her throat constricted. Her chest grew tight and she felt as if the floor might fall out from under her at any second. With her heart racing in her chest, she looked at her mother, her eyes wide.

"The letters?" Meilan finally managed to choke out. She needed to know what had happened to all of those letters. *What if Jayden never got them? What if he did get them and he ignored them?* Meilan didn't know which of the two possibilities would leave her heartache worsened but she needed the truth.

The truth won't change anything, the cruel voice in the back of her mind whispered. *What if he got the letters and decided I wasn't worth the effort?*

Her mother feebly shook her head. "We never mailed a single one."

Meilan froze in place, a strangled gasp escaping her as she sat back down on the bed. Her world was spinning faster and faster. She felt as if she would throw up.

Jayden had never gotten a single one of my letters. Never. He doesn't know.

Getting to her feet, she clenched the scrapbook in one hand until her knuckles were white. She couldn't believe what her parents had done.

"Meilan, we didn't want to hurt you. It was for the best."

For the first time in many years, Meilan took a hard look at her mother. She could see how the stress of previous years had worn on the woman; the wrinkles around her dark almond-shaped eyes, the way her once shiny hair was now dull and turning gray. There were tears in her mother's eyes but there was a stubborn set to her jaw that Meilan had known all too well growing up.

"We did what we had to do because we care about you, Meilan. You know that I love you."

Meilan nodded, biting her lip for a moment. She could consider everything that her parents had ever done for her but right in that moment, all she could feel was the breaking of her heart all over again. She found it easy to believe that her father orchestrated the entire ordeal – he always did what he thought was best for the family. Meilan knew that more often than not, her father was right in his decisions.

Not this one, she thought as she ran a hand through her hair and blinked away tears.

"Mom, how could you?" Meilan's bottom lip quivered. If she had to guess who would betray her trust, it would have never been her mother.

Her mother reached for her, her hands falling short as Meilan took a step back from the hug.

"We only did what we thought was right. Your father and I have both lived difficult lives. We never wanted to see the same hardships pressed on you. Please understand, Meilan. We did what we could with the information we had at the time. If I had known how it would have worn on you all of these years later, I would have stepped in."

"I know," Meilan said with a soft sigh, reaching up to brush the tears away from her eyes. "I believe you but I wished you had told me sooner. So many things could have been different. What if he was my one real chance at happiness and love?"

"Your family loves you."

Meilan shook her head, clenching the scrapbook tight. "My family deceived me for years. I know you meant well, but you must understand that revelation is not easy. I thought that I could trust you. I've always come to you with everything, Mom. Everything. You chose to keep this from me as long as you did. You chose to break my heart all over again."

"Don't say that. You don't know what could have been."

"I may never get the chance to know either." Meilan looked at her mother, the wrinkles seeming to grow impossibly deeper from this conversation alone. "I love you, Mom. And I know you only wanted what's best for me but I need time to process all of this."

Meilan shook her head and brushed by her mother. If Jayden had known what was in their letters, her entire life could look different than it did at that moment. She was uninterested in hearing her mother's pleas and apologies. There was only one thing that she could do, one thing that made sense to her muddled mind.

She would book the earliest flight to New York City that she could, and she would find Jayden. She had to. They'd been apart for far too long.

Chapter Two

Cups and saucers clinked as Jayden stared blankly down at his decadent lobster dinner. The lavish cuisine looked and smelled amazing as always, but he'd lost his appetite the moment his fiancée began berating the waitress.

"You don't have to look so miserable, Jayden," Emma said, sighing after demanding her soup be replaced yet again because it was not exactly the right temperature. "We're getting married in six months. At least act like you enjoy being around me."

Jayden cleared his throat and tried to muster up a smile for his wife-to-be. There'd been a time when he and Emma enjoyed each other's company, Jayden was sure of that. He just couldn't remember how long ago that was. If he were being honest, he couldn't pinpoint when everything started to fall apart either. It all blended together until it was a tangled mess, unable to be unraveled.

He supposed that their love for each other had started the day that she first waltzed into his life. Emma was bright and otherworldly. There was something about her that drew people to her. He had seen it the moment that she sat down beside him at a bar one night and asked how long he was going to wait before he bought her a drink.

Confidence. Charisma. The two things that he needed more of in his life were sitting wrapped in a perfect package beside him and asking for a drink.

The least he could do was order her a glass of wine.

After that first night together, he was a goner. It didn't take long for her to take hold on his heart. She was there through the worst moments of his life. The days where it seemed like trying to make something of himself was impossible. Emma made sure that he was in front of the right people at the right time. She placed him in positions of power and he liked it. They seemed like the kind of couple who were going to rule the city together. The ones who had both money and love.

There were days when he wondered where she would be without the beauty and the money she was accustomed to.

During other days, his mind flashed back to the painful weeks spent in the hospital shortly after they first said the three little words that changed his life.

Jayden looked down at his torso, his hand drifting over where his kidneys were – almost a soothing gesture. The kidney infection then had been stopped early and brought back under control. Even then, the doctor had warned him that it would only be a matter of time before they started to fail. Sooner or later, he would need a transplant.

Shoving the thoughts from his mind, he looked over at Emma, a smile on his face. She had sat through it all with him. Every health scare, financial scare, and all of the other fears and triumphs that weaved through his adult life. In each one, she was there advocating or applauding from the sideline. A woman out of his league still willing to stand by his side.

Emma was beautiful, that fact couldn't be denied. She'd modeled for every magazine and walked every runway in this city but it was her honey-hued eyes that Jayden had been entranced by. They reminded him of a mesmerizing gaze from his past.

There was a part of Jayden that thought he would be able to move on from the woman who broke his heart. How foolish that thought had been. Instead, he spent every day staring into honey irises that reminded him of Meilan. His dreams were haunted by those eyes and when he woke, he only found the wrong woman staring back at him.

Meilan ripped his heart to shreds without a second thought. Not once did she ever tell him that she would be leaving New York. Instead, he went to school one day and she wasn't there. The next day, she still was nowhere to be found. At first, he had thought that she was sick. It was only after begging one of the secretaries for an answer that he found out she had moved to California. That was the day that he felt his heart break for the first and last time.

He couldn't believe that she had left him without a word. Jayden had always known that Meilan wasn't in love with him like he was with her – but that was his burden to carry. At the very least, they were friends. Or so he had thought. A friend would have told the other friend that they were moving across the country. Not Meilan though.

There was no clear memory of the last day that he had seen her. It could have been the day that he gave her the scrapbook but it could have also been the following Saturday. His memories were too blurred now to pick the exact moment she left him behind.

Time should have erased her from his memory. The hurt alone should have made him dedicated to getting over her. It did, for a few years. He dated; he never grew attached to any of those women though. Why? It all came down to one simple reason.

They weren't Meilan.

She was the only person in the world that called him Jay. The only person who seemed to care whether he lived or died in that foster home. Meilan was the one person who made sure that Jayden got his life on the right track.

He had hoped that she would have been by his side to see him succeed.

She had never contacted him again though. Over the years, he had considered reaching out to her. Although, it always seemed like the wrong time. There had to have been a reason why she left without telling him. A reason for her never saying goodbye. As much as he wanted to talk to her again, see her one more time, he couldn't handle the rejection. Not for a second time.

Abruptly, Emma snapped her fingers in front of Jayden's face. He looked at her, not sure when he had looked away. Her face was storm clouds and he was sure her temper was as hot as a lightning strike. Emma was many wonderful things but she also had a wicked temper when she wasn't the center of attention.

"Excuse me! We're having a conversation, Jayden. I want to add more floral centerpieces to our wedding display. My sister had hundreds of flowers at her wedding and you know I have to outdo her. What do you think?"

"I think that sounds expensive." Jayden chuckled. He could imagine the number of flowers filling the venue. If Emma had her way, there wouldn't be anywhere to walk. Everything had to be beautiful where she was concerned. It wasn't something that he normally minded. It was due to her affinity for collecting beautiful things that his home look like something out of a magazine.

Emma didn't find the comment funny. Her face pinched and her arms crossed over her chest. "It's not like you don't have enough money for it. You might just be the richest man in New York."

Jayden suppressed a sigh. With Emma, everything was about money. She'd never had to live in the basement of a high school or depend on a good friend's compassion to get by. Jayden might be a wealthy investor living in opulence now, but he could never forget how far he'd come or how hard he had to work to get to where he was. If it wasn't for Meilan, he'd very likely have either starved or have spent the rest of his days on the side of a street. He owed her everything.

Jayden's phone rang, temporarily putting Emma's tantrum to the side. He looked at the number, recognizing it as one from his office but not knowing who it might be. Normally, his staff didn't call him after hours. When he had taken over the company, he had set a rule in place to protect his private life: *not unless the building was on fire.*

"The building better be on fire," Jayden said the moment the call connected.

"Hello, Jayden." The woman on the other end of the line was speaking so fast that Jayden didn't even get a chance to return the greeting. "Something awful has happened. One of the businesses that you invest in, the local airline, it-" the woman's voice caught and she had to pause to clear her throat. "One of their planes has crash-landed outside the city. You have business partners that might have been on that flight."

Jayden's stomach twisted, the blood freezing in his veins. Surviving a plane crash was rare. At worst, one of his business partners could be dead. It would trigger a meeting of the board and a restructuring of the company. Though he was the primary shareholder and the CEO, he couldn't lose one of the majority shareholders backing him.

"How many people were on that flight?" Jayden asked, his voice strained.

"Not many," the woman said. "It was a small plane and it wasn't fully booked. Here, I've just been emailed a copy of the passenger manifest by one of our connections at the airline itself. I'll read the names to you."

Jayden listened intently as the woman read name after name, relief slowly pulsing through his entire body as each one passed without his recognition. Emma was pouting in her chair, pushing her lobster around on the plate as he kept the phone close. By now his food would have gone cold but he didn't care. He just needed to know that the shareholders were alright; his company needed them to be alright.

Finally, she read one name that had him stop. It was as if time seemed to freeze in place. Nothing was moving. Nothing was real. In that moment, he could feel ice flowing through his veins. His hands shook as the phone dropped. He fumbled, catching it quickly and bringing it back to his ear.

"Wait," he gasped. "Repeat that last name again."

"You mean Meilan? Meilan Chen? It doesn't sound familiar to me... is she at one of our other branches?"

Everything around him seemed to lose definition as he sank deeper into his chair. The world was falling away from him and there was nothing that he could do to stop it. He bit down, trying to stop the scream that threatened to escape him. His teeth connecting with the fleshy inside of his mouth and all he could taste was metal. Jayden grabbed a linen napkin and wiped his mouth, a stream of blood from where he had bit himself staining the once pristine fabric. He could hear the thudding of his heart in his chest; he could hear the rush of blood in his ears. The sound of the busy restaurant and the smell of the food faded away. All he could see was a plane plummeting to the ground and Meilan's lifeless body carelessly strewn beside it.

He knew without a doubt that Meilan, *his* Meilan, was that passenger. He could feel it in his soul.

"What is her condition?" he whispered. His throat was so

tight he could hardly get the words out. "Did our contact at the airline include any of that information?"

The woman went completely silent for so long that Jayden almost threw his phone with frustration, but then she whispered, "Her body was recovered from the wreckage. First responders can't be sure of her state, but she is unresponsive. They're airlifting her to Renford Memorial."

Without a word, Jayden hung up his phone. He lingered just long enough to grab his wallet out of his pocket and throw his credit card down on the table to cover the meal, and then he bolted out of the restaurant without saying anything else.

Emma was calling for him, demanding that he return to the table and finish the meal but he couldn't hear her. Nothing else mattered in that moment except getting to the hospital.

Meilan needed him, and Jayden had to be there for her.

Chapter Three

The hospital reeked of bleach and misery. People around him were crying while nurses talked on the phone. Jayden watched as loved ones clutched each other over battered and bruised bodies. He tried to beat away the sinking feeling in his heart that insisted he would be one of those pitiful loved ones soon.

Meilan is going to be fine. She didn't die. Meilan is going to be fine.

He repeated the chant over and over again in his mind, the only saving grace as he clutched the arms of the hard plastic chair until his knuckles were white.

There was a page over the system as another ambulance drove into the bay outside. The doors slid open and nurses barreled out of the doors, a trauma surgeon hot on their heels and tying up his paper gown.

A gurney hurtled by him. There was a paramedic on top of gurney, giving compressions while a small machine screamed. The person on the gurney barely looked like a person. Their skin

– what little he could see through the blood – was bruised and torn.

The surgeon took over, the paramedic falling to the side. Jayden wanted to look away but his eyes were locked on the scene before him. The nurses that went out with the paramedic were shouting commands at those in their way, pushing the gurney toward the other end of the waiting area.

That poor person, he thought as they raced by him, more nurses joining in on the run and shouting orders to those around them. It was only a moment after they rushed by him that he saw who it was on the bed.

Doors swung shut behind them as Jayden jolted to his feet. He rushed to the nurse station across the room. The woman in front of him was speaking rapidly into the phone and held up a single finger. Jayden gritted his teeth and shifted his weight from foot to foot. That was *his* Meilan on that stretched and he would be damned if he had to keep waiting here before he could get to her.

"Hello," the nurse finally said as she placed the phone back on the cradle. "How can I help you?"

"That woman that just came in on the stretcher. I need to see her. I need to know what is going on."

The nurse cocked an eyebrow. "I'm sorry but unless you are immediate family, I can't give you any of that information."

He stared at the nurse for a moment, not quite believing what he was hearing. His hands were shaking as he gripped the edge of the counter, trying to steady himself. Black dots danced across his vision. After blinking rapidly, the dots disappeared and he took a deep breath.

"I'm her husband," Jayden said before he knew what words were coming out of his mouth. His cheeks flamed but he gave a confident nod. "That's my wife. I got a call that there had been a plane crash and she was on it. I need to see her."

The nurse gave him a skeptical look but nodded and turned to the computer, her fingers tapping away at the keys. "Well, Meilan Chen is being rushed into emergency surgery. It appears that she has a broken rib, several other broken bones throughout her body, and some internal bleeding. After they are done dealing with the bleeding, she is looking at a few hours of sutures and resetting her bones. She will not be ready to have a visitor for a few hours."

"Is there somewhere that I can wait for her then? I want to be here when she wakes up."

The nurse gestured for another woman. "Ms. Chen is being checked into room 316. Please show her husband to the room where he can wait for her."

"Thank you," Jayden said, giving the nurse an easy smile. "I appreciate it."

The nurse smirked and nodded. "Remember, if any of the other nurses ask, you're her husband."

His mouth gaped open for a minute before he was led away by another nurse. *How did she know that I was lying?* Looking down at his hand, he noticed the absence of a ring. That wasn't uncommon these days though. More and more people were choosing not to wear a ring.

When he reached the room, he saw two beds. An elderly woman was sitting in one and yelling at the soap opera on the television. Jayden scowled and turned to the nurse.

"What can we do about getting Meilan a private room? She will need peace to recover."

The nurse sighed. "I'm not sure what you were expecting, sir. But this is what most of the rooms are like. If she is willing to pay more, then there are some private rooms but the price is quite steep."

Jayden pulled his wallet from his pocket and grabbed his other credit card. "I can cover all of the costs."

Within an hour, he had arranged for a private room for Meilan. The entirety of her medical bill would be charged to his card. As he sank down into the large recliner in the corner of the room, he was glad that he had never given Emma access to his bank accounts. She would throw a fit when she found out that he was paying for someone else's medical stay.

It wasn't a conversation he was looking forward to having with her.

At close to three in the morning, Meilan was wheeled in on another stretched. Jayden wiped the sleep from his eyes and watched as she was transferred from one bed to another. Tubes ran from her body to a series of machines, the beep quiet but steady. Her body looked too small, tiny, as if she was nothing more than a whisp of a girl.

"You're her husband?" the doctor said as she finished connecting a tube to another machine. "I'm Dr. Moore."

"Yes," Jayden said as he stood up and ran a hand along his jaw. "What's wrong with Meilan? Is she going to be okay?"

The doctor grabbed a little stool and pulled it over to where Jayden stood, motioning for him to sit back down. Once he was seated, she flipped open the cover on her tablet. He watched as her fingers flew over the screen.

"She is very lucky. There are only two other survivors from that crash and they are in a much worse state." The doctor didn't have to tell him about the several others that died. He already knew they were gone and he couldn't get the thought out of his head that it could have been Meilan.

"So, she's okay?" He twisted his hands together, trying to keep his eyes on the doctor and off of Meilan. *What is she even doing in New York?*

Dr. Moore shook her head, a sad smile spreading over her face. "I'm afraid that is not how I would phrase it. You see, while she did survive the crash, there was still an extensive amount of damage done to her body. She has a broken rib and a fractured ankle. Her entire body is covered in lesions and bruises. A few blood vessels in her eyes have popped but those should heal relatively quickly. What I am concerned about is her brain."

Jayden felt his heart drop through his stomach and to the floor. When there were problems with the brain or the heart the news was rarely good. He had seen enough to know that much. Jayden buried his face in his shaking hands for a second, taking deep breaths and trying to still his racing heart. Bile rose in his throat as his stomach tossed and turned.

"What do you mean," he finally said, his words slow and measured. "That it's her brain you're worried about?"

"She has gone into a coma. It is not medically-induced which means that we have no way of knowing when she will come out of it."

Jayden held up a hand, stopping the doctor before she could say more. "Wait, what does that mean? I know what a coma is but what does it mean if we don't know when she will wake up?"

"The brain goes into a coma to protect itself and the rest of the body from traumatic events. Usually, this is a good thing. It allows the body to heal without having to process any extra stimuli. However, in some cases, the brain shuts too far down. Kind of like a switch has been flipped but once it was off, somebody ripped the switch out of the wall."

He nodded, the color draining from his face. "What happens if she doesn't wake up?"

Dr. Moore closed the tablet and leaned forward, clasping one of his hands with hers. He looked at the difference between their skin tones, thinking that few would think to touch him. He was an imposing black male. People were afraid of him. Yet, here was this woman who was no bigger than his thumb whose first thought was to comfort him.

"Your wife may never wake up. There is no way of knowing how the coma will affect her body. Because she is currently being sustained with life support, you and I need to discuss her wishes. I know this is a difficult time, but it is important that we follow Meilan's wishes."

Jayden rubbed his hands down his face, sighing heavily. "I don't know. It was never something we really talked about."

He glanced at the machines again. What would Meilan want? She had always been so happy, so full of life. Would she want to spend an indeterminate amount of time linked up to machines and confined to a bed?

Jayden stood up and started pacing from one side of the room to the next. It wasn't his decision to make. He would hire a private investigator to find her mother. She could make the decision for Meilan. It wasn't his place.

Finally, Jayden looked at the doctor. "I'm sorry. I have no clue how to answer that at all."

Dr. Moore stood up and nodded. "I will leave you and your wife now. Nurses will be in every few hours to check on her state. You and I can discuss her wishes again in a few days."

Jayden looked at Meilan lying helpless in the hospital bed and breathed a sigh of defeat. "Alright."

He watched as Dr. Moore left the room before he walked to Meilan's beside. Tubes ran all over her body, peeking out from between the bandages and running to the machines. His heart was pounding in his chest as he gently touched her hand. It was cold to the touch and limp.

"Come on, Meilan. You need to pull through this." He smiled and smoothed her hair away from her face. "You and I need to have a very long conversation about breaking hearts. We can't do that if you are in a coma."

He laughed to himself and touched her hand once more

before stepping away. There was nothing he wouldn't do for her. Nothing. Jayden took a seat in the recliner, making himself comfortable once more. It would be a long night of worrying.

Chapter Four

"Where the hell did you go last night?" Emma stood in the doorway to their bedroom, her arms crossed and her lips pursed. "You left me at the restaurant. You walked out on me when we were supposed to be discussing wedding plans. And then you don't come home all night? What is going on Jayden?"

He didn't answer her, instead brushing by her to fall onto their bed and close his eyes. Sleep was a foreigner to him. The most sleep he had gotten last night was maybe an hour between rounds of nurses storming into the room and checking Meilan's vitals. Each time they had entered the room, he had woken up. It seemed as if his mind was prepared to hear the worst and when it didn't come, he found himself thinking of all of the other things that could have happened.

"Jayden? What is going on with you lately?"

Jayden groaned into the pillow before rolling onto his back to stare at the ceiling. "An old friend of mine was on the plane that crashed yesterday."

"Oh no, how is he? Is he alive?" The irritation had melted

from Emma's voice as she came to sit beside him, her hand resting on his thigh. Jayden glanced at her and for a moment, she was the same woman that he had fallen in love with three years ago.

"He's alive but pretty beat up. In addition to all of the physical injuries, there's the coma to consider too." In that moment, Jayden had never been more disgusted with himself. If there was one thing that he prided himself on, it was his honesty. Now here he was telling his fiancée that the woman lying in a bed he was paying for was a man. Emma would never understand the feelings running through Jayden, especially if she knew it was a woman. All Emma would see would be red.

Emma's hand drifted softly on his thigh. "Well, you get some rest. You look exhausted. Are you going to be going back there tonight? You hate hospitals since the infection. Do you need me to go with you?"

Jayden nodded, closing his eyes once more. "Yeah, I'm going to get some rest and then I'm heading back for a bit. He doesn't have any family here and I hate the thought of him waking up and nobody he knows being there. Don't worry about coming with me though. I'll be okay and you have some wedding plans to handle. I know things go smoother if I'm not in your way anyway."

Another lie. Maybe Meilan did have family here now. It had been a long time since they had last seen each other. Who knew what was going on in her life now? He certainly didn't. Jayden looked down at his hands, his eyes burning with the tears he forced himself to hold back. He should have found the money and followed her family to the other side of the country. In his mind, he should have done all that he could to make sure that their relationship had survived.

Maybe if it had, she wouldn't be lying in a hospital bed and fighting for her life.

Jayden glanced at Emma. Her eyebrows were furrowed and a small frown was on her face. She reached out to smooth a hand along his jaw. He sighed, leaning into the familiar touch that had comforted him countless times before. Jayden wanted to sit there, to soak in her sympathy and have someone around to tell him that it would be okay. Instead, he pulled away from her. He couldn't be relying on Emma when he was lying to her about what was happening. It would only hurt her to know the truth. He loved her. The last thing he wanted to do was hurt her.

"I can only imagine," Emma said as she stood up and smoothed out her skirt. "On a plane one minute and in a hospital the next. That would be terrifying. If you're sure you don't need me there, then I'll go out and look at some more wedding things. You let me know if you need me, okay? We do have to go cake tasting tomorrow though, so make sure you meet me at the venue for six, okay?"

"I'll be there." Jayden grabbed her hand and pulled her down to place a quick kiss on her lips. As difficult as she was, he loved her and everything that they had been through together. Meilan appearing in his life once more wouldn't make things complicated – it couldn't. He loved Emma and he was going to marry her.

"I'm serious," she whispered, her honey eyes searching his. "You let me know if you need anything and I'll be there."

He smiled and nodded. "I know, honey. You always have been there for me. I'm a big boy though. And there's not much to do in the hospital when someone is conscious, let alone when they are in a coma."

Emma chuckled and stood up. "Alright. You need me, you call. If not, I'll see you at the cake tasting."

"Love you," Jayden said, though the words left a slightly bitter taste in his mouth.

He waited until he heard Emma's car leave before he got to

his feet and headed to the shower. The scent of the hospital clung to him in a way that reminded Jayden too much of his childhood. More nights than he even cared to try and count had been spent in the hospital after more than one foster parent had lashed out.

Once he was showered and dressed, he walked downstairs to the kitchen. A few minutes later, he was walking through the library with a sandwich in one hand and pulling books that Meilan would like down with the other. When he had been teaching her English in high school, he had read *Peter Pan* to her more times than he could count.

Jayden walked over to a bookshelf in the back of his library where the beat-up copy he used to read her lived inside a glass showcase. Emma always asked why a cheap thrift store edition was preserved. Whenever she asked, Jayden would tell her it was the only thing that he had taken from foster home to foster home with him. Though it wasn't a lie, it wasn't the truth either. That book was the only piece of Meilan that he had been able to hold onto through the last thirteen years.

With a sigh, he sat down on a couch and thumbed through the book, looking at all of the creases and the tiny tears. Thirteen years had passed since he had last seen her. They were thirty now and everything about their lives had changed.

After a few more moments of thinking about the way the sunlight shone in her hair while they read by the river, he took the book and went to his car. It was time to go see the one woman who still had an inexplicable hold over his heart.

When he arrived at the hospital, the nurse was just leaving Meilan's room. Jayden walked in and pulled the recliner closer to the bed. Leaning back, he opened up the book and began reading. It had been thirteen years since he had last read to her like this, since he had last taken a moment to read a book and relax.

At first, starting the book was difficult. It had been years since he had last read to anyone and well over a decade since he had last read this book. Sure, he had collected several copies over the years – another thing that Emma never understood and he never told her the truth about – but he could never bring himself to read them.

After an hour of reading, his voice grew hoarse and another nurse came in. While she checked over Meilan, Jayden headed to the courtyard to make his call.

The courtyard was beautiful. Big bushes of roses bloomed along the paths and there was bright green grass in large patches. It was peaceful, a place for patients and families to relax and feel as if they were far away from the hospital for a few moments.

Jayden pulled his phone from his pocket and dialed the number of his private investigator. It rang for a long time; Jayden was certain that he would reach Kevin's voicemail. The man preferred to screen his calls and only return the ones that he deemed important enough for his time. Jayden couldn't blame him; in Kevin's line of work time was money.

"Hello," Kevin said, his voice gruff. "What do you want?"

Jayden chuckled. "Is that any way to talk to one of your oldest friends?"

"Yeah, sure. The child that I kept arresting. One of my oldest friends? Unlikely."

"I turned out decent," Jayden said as he walked further from the hospital.

"Only because that little Chinese girl whipped you into shape. You'd probably be dead now if it weren't for her."

Jayden knew that much was true. "Anyways, listen. I need you to track down Ling Chen."

"Any idea on her last known location?"

"New York thirteen years ago?" Jayden grinned as Kevin

groaned and cussed him out. "Calm down, old man. Last I knew of, she was in California. I don't have more specifics though."

"Unique enough name," Kevin said after a moment. "Is there a reason I need to be aware of?"

"Make contact with her, if you will. Her daughter is in Redford Hospital after being involved in a plane crash."

"And what if this woman doesn't want to hear anything about her daughter? You know as well as I do that there are families who want nothing to do with each other," Kevin said, the sound of rustling in the background of the call. Jayden hoped that the man was in the middle of booking his plane ticket.

"I've known her family since I was a teenager. They're not that kind of family." Jayden sighed and looked around, desperately wanting something to do with his hands while he spoke but finding nothing. "She and her mother are close. Always have been."

Kevin paused for a moment. "If you know her family that well, why aren't you the one getting in contact with her mother? Not that I mind the extra pay, but it would probably be better coming from you."

Jayden rubbed his jaw, staring at a bird that sat in a tree not far away from him. "Trust me. It's better if I'm not the one to contact them. Her family and I have a messy history at best."

"They hate you. Got it."

Jayden laughed and shook his head. It was hard to believe that he was on friendly terms with the man that used to throw him into jail. "I don't know if they hate me or not. I haven't seen them since I was seventeen and even back then, we weren't overly friendly. But I think that I am the last person they would want to hear from – if they even remember me."

"Alright, well, I'll be landing in California tomorrow and tracking down Mrs. Chen. I'll let you know once I've made contact."

"Thank you, Kevin."

"Not a problem, kid. You know that you can count on me."

The call ended and Jayden slipped the phone back into his pocket. He turned his face to the sun, soaking in the rays for a few moments before wandering back to the hospital. After Meilan had left, Jayden had started getting into more trouble. More than once Kevin had arrested Jayden, waiting with him until his social worker had shown up. Jayden would be released, hole up in his tiny little apartment for a few days, go to school, and then get into trouble again. It was after the seventh or eighth arrest that Kevin got personally involved.

Kevin was the only father-figure that Jayden had ever known. Instead of getting into trouble after school, Kevin would force him to come to the station and study or work. He spent hours doing community service in exchange for wiping his record clean. Without Kevin, Jayden never would have gone to university or become the successful man he was now. Kevin had been the first one to storm through the doors when Jayden was hospitalized for his kidneys. Hell, Jayden was pretty sure Kevin's demanding and abrupt nature had caused at least one doctor to quit. He owed everything to Kevin and Meilan. Now, one of them was in a hospital bed and there was no promise of her living.

When Jayden walked back into the room, Meilan was as unchanged as ever. Her skin was a sickly pale color and the shine was gone from her hair. Jayden grabbed *Peter Pan* and sat back in the chair. It was odd to read to an empty room but there was nothing he could do about it. There would be no smile from Meilan when they finally reached Neverland or encouragement to go on when he felt like stopping. Instead, there was only the steady beeping of the machines. Nothing else.

He read until his voice was hoarse, only stopping to get a drink of water before he continued reading. Hours passed, his feet up on the edge of her bed as he thumbed through the well-loved pages. Though he wasn't sure if she knew what was going on around her, he had heard that people in comas might hear. When he turned another page, he decided that he would keep reading to her until she woke.

"Come on, Meilan," he whispered when he took a break to get food. "You love stories. If anything is going to wake you up, it's going to be the books."

He squeezed her hand and went into the hallway. It was a miracle that she had survived but there was still a long road of healing in front of her and that was only if she woke up. Jayden rubbed his eyes, blinking away the tears that started to form.

You have to pull through Meilan, you just have to.

Chapter Five

Emma clutched Jayden's arm as they walked into the ballroom of the *Empire Resort*. He looked down at the cherry red nails digging into his grey sleeve. Her grip was too tight to be considered normal and he found himself wondering what he had done wrong this time. It seemed like he was always doing something wrong where Emma was concerned.

Even when he said and did everything right, she still found a problem to point out. Something that wasn't quite up to her standards. If he were being honest, there were times that the small voice in the back of his mind wondered if she only started dating him to show her family what a child from a broken home could become. It would make a great narrative for years to come — always to be brought up at family dinners and big events.

How do you know that your relationship is doomed? he thought as they were greeted by a woman who couldn't keep her eyes to herself. Jayden looked at her, offering a small smile, but there were only two thoughts that could possibly be going through her head. The first? What is this man doing here? The second? I wonder what his net worth is.

Looking back at Emma, he plastered on a bigger smile, reminding himself that this was her day and that they had been planning it for a while. They had gone through all of the motions of starting a life together. He knew that there was love between them but lately it felt like instead of a romantic love, they were borderline platonic.

What if I am settling for her? He looked at the beautiful woman on his arm and sighed, the smile dropping.

Emma had been his first love after Meilan. She had wanted a future with him – one that involved a lot of money. However, they were too absent from each other's lives. Most nights, they didn't share a bed. They hadn't in months. It was easier to maintain separate homes. She would come and go as she pleased – often travelling for work – and he would work late nights and early mornings. Their lifestyles barely accommodated each other.

Through all of the ups and downs in the last few years, Jayden had run to Emma. She had become his family, filling a void in his heart that he hadn't realized was quite that big. She nestled there and made him feel whole. Loved. Important to somebody. Like maybe his life was worth living after all.

He hadn't felt that way since Meilan.

Jayden followed Emma to the table and took the seat beside her as trays of tiny cake slices were placed in front of them. The woman and Emma started talking about all of the details of the wedding – most of which were lost on Jayden. He supposed it would be better to be more involved in his own wedding but he didn't think that Emma would want it that way. As long as she had access to his credit cards, she didn't care about much else.

"What do you think about the chocolate one with the rose icing?" Emma asked as she motioned her fork toward a chocolate cake smothered in pink icing.

Jayden took a bite and wrinkled his nose. Swallowing the

cake was difficult at best. "That's not bad," he said, grabbing his napkin to wipe his mouth. "But it might not be something that the majority of our guests enjoy. It is definitely more of an acquired taste."

Emma frowned. "I don't care what everyone else likes. This is my wedding and it will have whatever cake I want it to have."

Jayden plastered on a smile and squeezed her hand. "Of course it will, babe, but I think that we should also consider what will happen if you serve this cake and somebody doesn't like it."

"My sister would hate it just to start and argument," Emma said as she stabbed a piece of vanilla cake with lemon icing. "Then she would tell all of our guests that it made her sick. She would definitely make it her mission to ruin my wedding."

"Exactly," Jayden said before taking a bite of the lemon cake as well. "I like this one. It's light and refreshing. Perfect for a summer wedding."

Emma beamed at him and nodded. "Exactly what I was thinking. Everybody will love it. Now, how many tiers do you think we will need?"

"Well, the number of tiers will depend on the number of guests you have," the woman said as she grabbed a clipboard and a pen from somewhere underneath the table. "How many guests were there going to be?"

"Over two hundred. Quite possibly over three hundred," Emma said.

It was at that moment that Jayden started losing interest in where the conversation was heading. In his opinion, the guest count was far too high. He had wanted a simple wedding with some of their closest friends and her family. Instead, their special day was turning into a circus of epic proportions.

Jayden looked at Emma, reaching beneath the table to rest his hand on her thigh. She looked back at him with a bright smile that could melt icebergs. He grinned back at her, finally seeing a reflection of the woman that he had fallen in love with. It was that smile that reminded him exactly why they were getting married in the first place. He loved her just like she loved him.

After a few more hours of discussing details with the wedding planner, Emma and Jayden left their venue. They walked down the street; their fingers intertwined. He grinned as Emma told him all about their wedding. Things were different when she was this happy. Things felt more normal than they had in a long time.

"Thank you for being here today," Emma said as she leaned her head against his shoulder for a moment. "It means a lot. I know that you aren't as excited about the wedding as I am but lately it feels like you've been completely checked out of our relationship."

"You know I love you," Jayden said. "I just never understood the point of getting married. Why do we need a paper to tell us that we plan to spend our lives together?"

With a laugh, Emma shook her head. "I know that you'll never understand it but the show we put on for our peers and my family is important. If my wedding isn't the best in New York, I'm giving all of the other women in the city permission to walk all over me. There is no way that is going to happen. Money is status in this city, Jayden. My wedding is going to be better than anyone else's."

Jayden nodded, knowing it was the only response that he could give at that moment. He had only proposed and wanted a wedding because he knew it was what Emma wanted. Even though it wasn't what he should be doing, he was remaking himself to fit the image that she wanted him to be. Basic survival skills resurfacing.

Marriage wasn't in his life plan – not since Meilan left him. Even then, any thought of marriage would have sent him running for the hills. Look what marriage had done to all of the other foster children he had lived with. More often than not, the marriage was followed by divorce. Divorce was quickly followed by removal of children from their homes.

What would happen if he married someone? Would he be doomed to repeat the same cycle that all of the children he had seen growing up had gone through?

Shaking his head, he tried to distance them from his thoughts. He didn't want to know what all of this would mean if he gave himself time to truly think it through.

"I have to go back to the hospital tonight," Jayden said as their car pulled up alongside the curb. Emma got in and rolled the window down.

"Is your friend okay?"

"About as good as can be expected," Jayden said with a shrug. "I'll try to make it home to see you for a little bit tomorrow morning but I have taken time off of work until his family can get here to look after him."

"You are a good man," Emma said. "I love you. See you later."

"You too," Jayden said, knocking on the roof of the car. He watched as the car pulled away from the curb and entered the New York traffic.

The hospital wasn't far from where he was. It made more sense to walk and try to clear his head than to wait for another car. The walk alone would give him time to think about what he would say to Meilan's mother. How do you tell someone that their child may die?

When Jayden entered Meilan's room that afternoon, the machines started shrieking. He raced to her beside and slammed his hand against the red call button, tears burning in his eyes. Jayden's hands were shaking at his sides, stepping back as doctors and nurses raced into the room.

Jayden watched as they shouted to each other, one man grabbing a needle while another woman opened Meilan's gown. He averted his eyes and backed into a corner as they pulled paddles off a cart.

"Clear!" one woman yelled. He couldn't help himself, he had to look. *What if this is the last time that I ever see her?*

Jayden saw Meilan's body jerk on the bed but the machines kept screaming. Over and over again they shocked her until the rhythm became steady once more. The nurses covered her back up as Dr. Moore entered the room.

The floor felt like it was falling away beneath him. He was drowning and there was no life preserver for him to grab on to. Jayden was stuck to the sidelines, watching Meilan fight for her life and unable to do anything about it. Rage boiled his blood, his hands becoming fists at his sides.

"Status?" Dr. Moore grabbed Meilan's charts from one of the machines and looked at the lines. None of the words the nurses and doctor said made sense to Jayden. His head spun as he looked at his friend, helpless on the bed.

After a few more minutes, all of the other people left the room. Dr. Moore looked at him and nodded to the recliner. Jayden took a seat, his eyes wide as he reached forward and grabbed Meilan's hand. Her skin was unusually cool. His fingertips rested on her wrist, searching for a pulse. He had to confirm it for himself; the beeping of the machines doing little to soothe his fear. After a few moments of shallow breathing while he waited, he felt her pulse. It was faint and seemed to be growing fainter, but it was there.

There's still hope yet, he thought as he blinked back tears.

"You and I are going to have to have that talk about your wife's wishes soon."

Jayden nodded, his thumb drifting across the back of Meilan's cold hand. "I know. I have someone getting in contact with her mother. Once I've spoken to her there should be a better idea of what is going on."

"I know this isn't easy," Dr. Moore said as she pulled over the little stool and sat down once again. "But the truth is that your wife may not recover from the trauma. It is something that you have to consider."

"I have been considering it!" Jayden's voice raised higher than he intended. He looked down at Meilan before rubbing the back of his neck. The room felt as if it was getting hotter and the walls were closing in. "I'm sorry."

"Don't be," Dr. Moore said as she reached out to squeeze his shoulder. "This is a hard time for you as well. Your wife is in pain and there is nothing that you can do about it. She is suffering and you want to change that but you can't. The only solace is that her brain is keeping her unconscious for most of this. Now, we can wait for her mother but I would advise strongly that you start thinking about what is best for her."

Jayden nodded, his thumb still drifting over Meilan's hand. "Is she okay?"

Dr. Moore frowned. "There isn't anything that can tell us what just happened. All we know is that her heart started failing but we were able to bring her back this time. You need to consider what will happen in the event that we can't bring her back."

"I'll think about it," Jayden said, his voice wavering as he squeezed Meilan's hand. "I'll talk to her mother and I'll think about it."

Dr. Moore stood up and walked to the door. "Let the nurses know if there is anything that you need."

"Will do," Jayden said.

Once the doctor was gone, he got into the bed beside Meilan, careful to avoid all of the wires and tubes. He linked his hands behind his head and stared up at the ceiling. Kicking off his shoes, he made himself comfortable. Meilan was so tiny that there was more than enough room for both of them. For a moment, he was reminded of when they used to lay beside each other under the stars in the summer and talk about all of their hopes and dreams.

"You know, Meilan, I couldn't believe that you just left me like that. Odd now that you have returned to my life after all this time. I think that is the way that it is meant to be, you know? Something brought us back together after all this time."

He sighed and closed his eyes for a few seconds. Jayden focused on deep breaths, trying to forget that they were in a hospital. In his mind, he could see them counting the stars together and talking about all of the things that their futures would hold. They spent hours talking over where they would go to school and what they would do with their lives. Meilan's dreams were always so much bigger than his own.

She used to say that she would go to school to become a social worker. A little social justice warrior if he ever saw one. Though she had never been told everything about his past – he had hidden the more disturbing parts from her – she had always insisted that she wanted to make sure no children went through what he did.

"Where did you end up in life?" he whispered as he opened his eyes to look at her. It was then that he saw Emma standing in the doorway to the hospital room with a bouquet of flowers in her hand.

Jayden saw the glassy look in her eyes as she stared at the body on the bed. He could only imagine what was going through her head in that moment. The glaringly obvious fact was that he had lied about what most would consider a very important fact. She would be running through everything else that had happened since Meilan arrived in the hospital and she would be crafting the story that made the most sense to her.

If he had to guess, the story that Emma came up with wouldn't be too far from the truth.

"What is going on?" Her voice wavered as she spoke, the flowers dropping to the floor.

Jayden leapt out of the bed. "Emma, what are you doing here?"

She scoffed and her eyes narrowed into a sharp glare. "That's your response to being caught in bed with another woman?"

"First of all," Jayden said, his temper flaring up and his jaw clenching. "I am not in bed with her or sleeping with her or any of that."

"You told me that it was a man that was in the plane crash. I know that hospitals scare you. I know that you would rather not be here alone – especially if your friend is dying. I know that you're going to need someone by your side. So, I come here with flowers, trying to be supportive. I sweet-talk the nurse at the front desk and she tells me where you are. And then I come up here and find you in bed with another woman!"

"Calm down and lower your voice. This is a hospital and people are trying to heal. They don't need to hear all about your insecurities." He grimaced. The last thing he wanted to do was dismiss the valid feelings she was having – after all, he had lied – however he didn't want to get kicked out of Meilan's room. His being in that room was dependent on the nurses believing Meilan was his wife.

Emma scoffed and stomped over to him, stopping when they were toe-to-toe. "Who do you think you are? Telling me to calm down?"

"You are overreacting. Meilan is my oldest friend. She pulled me out of a very dark hole and if it weren't for her, I wouldn't be standing here in front of you. So, here is what is going to happen. You are going to be mad all you want and that is not going to change anything. I will continue to sit by Meilan's side until she no longer needs me. I am not cheating on you. I love you. But my friend needs me right now. You don't have to like that I am here or even understand why, but you are not going to come in here and throw a fit about it."

Emma looked stunned for a moment, stumbling back a second. He was no longer the Jayden that she had always known. The Jayden she knew was soft spoken and rarely angered. He never once raised his voice to her. Tears welled in her eyes as she stepped away.

"Fine. I'll see you at home. If you even remember where that is anymore."

"I remember." *If you are talking about the home we haven't lived in together in months.* He wanted to argue with her, scream and shout as if it would relieve all of his frustration with the entire ordeal. Instead, he pressed his lips shut.

Jayden watched as Emma spun on her heel and walked out of the room. With a sigh, he slumped into the recliner and pinched the bridge of his nose. That could not have gone any worse.

A cheery sound rang through the room, coming from deep within Jayden's pocket. With a sigh, he pulled the phone out and slid his thumb across the screen.

"Hello?"

"It's Kevin. I'm with Mrs. Chen and she would like to speak with you about her daughter."

Jayden sighed. This was the part that he wasn't looking forward to at all. "Alright. Put her on and thank you, Kevin."

"Where is my daughter?" Mrs. Chen's voice was thin and strained, as if she had been crying and had no more energy to go on. Her accent was still there but it was no longer as strong as it had been when Jayden and Meilan had been growing up.

"I'm with her right now. We're at Ray Memorial Hospital in New York. It's one of the best in the country."

"How can she afford that?" Mrs. Chen said, her voice becoming sharp. "Meilan doesn't make enough to be able to care for herself like that. Social work doesn't pay that well. I don't have the money to provide that kind of care for her either. How did she get to such a place?"

Jayden paused for a moment. This was not the woman he remembered speaking on the phone. Mrs. Chen was meek. She didn't raise her voice. Maybe her daughter was finally wearing off on her.

A small smile crossed Jayden's face as he looked at Meilan. *So, she did become a social worker after all.* "I'm paying for it."

"No," Mrs. Chen said. "We do not take charity."

"It's not charity. I owe her the life I have now and paying for her hospital care is the least that I can do. However, that is not why I asked Kevin to find you."

"Is Meilan alive – rather is she going to stay alive?" The strength left Mrs. Chen's voice. Instead, it was soft and gentle, more like the meek woman he remembered though there was still worry there. Who could blame her for her initial reaction? She had just found out that her daughter was dying in a hospital.

"Yes, at least I hope so but that is what I want to talk to you about."

There was a long pause on the other end of the line, followed by strangled breathing. "What do you mean? She is alive, but what?"

"The doctors want to know what to do. As it stands right now, she is on life support and in a coma. There is no way of knowing if she will pull through. They want to discuss how long to keep her on life support for."

The other end of the phone went completely silent. Jayden couldn't even hear Mrs. Chen breathing. For a moment, he wondered if she had hung up on him. He pulled his phone away from his face and checked the screen. The call was still going.

"Mrs. Chen? I know this is difficult to consider, but the doctors do need an answer. Would Meilan want to be kept on life support despite all odds?"

"You must understand, making this decision is hard over the phone. How am I supposed to decide whether my daughter lives or dies from the other side of the country?" Mrs. Chen's sobs tore Jayden's heart in two.

"I will buy you a ticket to bring you here. I have a couple of different properties you could stay in." Jayden paused, wondering if she would consider this charity as well. "Let me help you in case she doesn't make it."

There was another strangled sob. "I can't come. I can't. My husband and I own a shop here – herbal medicine – and there is nobody to run it since he died. None of our family is here and I can't trust just anyone to know what to prescribe to clients. There is also the matter of the stroke I suffered not long ago. My doctors are concerned about blog clots. I am forbidden from flying or driving long distances in case a clot forms and travels to my heart. I would be there this second if I could."

"I understand. I am sorry to hear about your stroke. I hope that one day you are fully recovered from it." Jayden's hand clenched into a fist at his side. After a moment, he flexed his hand, releasing the tension. Meilan's mother would be here if she could, he knew that. No parent would willingly stay on the other side of the country while their daughter was in a coma.

"This is terrible. A mother's worst nightmare," Mrs. Chen said with another sob. "I can't be there for my baby."

"I'll take good care of her, I promise."

"And yet, you are telling me that I must be the one to decide whether my daughter lives or dies," she said with a dark chuckle, followed by another broken sob. "I know it is my decision."

"What would Meilan want?"

"I don't know what she would want." There was a deep, wavering breath. Her voice when she next spoke was softer than before, a sense of resignation taking over. It was a harsh reality that no parent should ever have to face. "I suppose that she wouldn't want to live the rest of her life connected to machines."

Jayden nodded, reaching out to hold Meilan's hand, his thumb drifting over the back of it as he spoke to her mother. "I understand. She was far too lively when we were younger to want to live like this. It's not living. It's just being kept alive."

"I want to give her a fighting chance. Give her another two weeks. If she doesn't pull through after that, then I will get on a plane and I will come there. I cannot leave California right now. There is too much going on here. To think, the last time that I saw her was when she came to get that little scrapbook you gave her."

"She still has that?"

"Yes," Mrs. Chen said before pausing for a moment. "There is something else that I feel that I should tell you, Jayden. The first being that I owe you an apology."

"An apology?" He sat down on the edge of the bed, his fingers tightening around Meilan's. "I don't think that I understand."

Mrs. Chen sighed. "I fear that my husband and I were rather prejudiced against you. Well, your relationship with Meilan to be more exact. You see, an interracial relationship was not what we wanted for our daughter. Well, not what my husband wanted for her. As his wife, I was expected to support him in his decisions for our family, even if I thought that they were wrong. You have to understand, my problem was never with you. I had never seen my daughter happier than when she was with you. The guilt of what we did has been tearing away at me for years. Of course, it is not your job to absolve my guilt. I just want you to know that I am sorry, and if you two try to start a relationship once more, I will not stand in the way. All I want is for Meilan to be happy."

Jayden stiffened, dropping Meilan's hand and his own balling into a fist. It was a lot of information to take in all at once. His mind was racing, trying to process it all but the only thing that came to mind to say was, "Oh?"

"I am sorry. It was a perspective that we were brought up with. A very wrong one, as I have come to learn. We moved away to prevent you two from growing closer. I have carried that regret with me for many years."

"Well, I can't say that your thoughts on the matter are okay, because they're not. I have done nothing wrong to you or your family but you viewed me as a threat because of the color of my skin. However, I do appreciate the honesty."

He gritted his teeth, the words tasting bitter in his mouth. Meilan had moved away because her parents – specifically her father - didn't want to see a Chinese woman with an African-American man. If Meilan's mother just wanted her to be happy, why didn't she intervene? Now, it was years later and they both had other lives to live. A lump rose in his throat, threatening to choke him as he relaxed his hand and clenched it again.

"There is something else," Mrs. Chen said. "I have a pile of letters Meilan wrote to you. Nearly every single day for a year. My husband wanted to throw the letters out but I have kept them and I would like to send them to you. I meant to give them to her when she found the scrapbook but she was not interested in listening to anything that I had to say at that time. If I send them to you with Kevin, will you give them to her? Tell her that I love her and I will support her no matter what."

Jayden didn't know what else to say to her. "I would like that very much."

"I am sorry for all the problems that we have caused between you too. If I thought that you and Meilan would be together again, thirteen years later, I may have urged my husband to stay in New York. We were wrong and I know that nothing I can ever say to you will make up for the racism that we have directed your way."

There was something in her tone that made him think that she wasn't asking for forgiveness. He hoped that she understood how wrong that she had been. How misinformed and biased. All of his years being judged by others told him that it would be her actions that determined whether she was changing or not.

"If you want to talk about Meilan or how things are going, just ask Kevin for my number and he will give it to you."

"Thank you," Mrs. Chen said. "I will send the letters back with Kevin."

"Goodbye, Mrs. Chen."

"Goodbye."

The call ended and Jayden was left staring at the phone. After a few moments, he twisted in place to look at Meilan. Everything that had gone wrong after she left was starting to fall into place. For years, he had thought that she had abandoned him and didn't care about their friendship enough to get in contact. Instead, she had been trying but her parents had been standing in their way.

Mrs. Chen stood in their way just as much as her husband, even if she said that the idea was largely his. Even if she never personally had a problem, she had still allowed her husband's racist thoughts to permeate their lives. Two adults ruined their happiness over skin color.

Jayden felt sick to his stomach knowing the true reason for their leaving and why he had never heard from Meilan again. It hadn't been for lack of her trying. Instead, it was because he had never received the letters and both of them were left feeling like the other person didn't care anymore.

What a way for our lives to have gone.

As he sat looking at her, he wondered what would have happened if he had gotten those letters. Would they be together now? Instead of seeing Emma walk down the aisle in a month, it could have been Meilan. He rubbed his face, the energy draining from his body. There were too many variables to think of all that could have been. He was marrying Emma. That was the end of the story. He would watch his beautiful bride walk down the aisle and they would be together for the rest of their lives. Maybe he and Meilan could be friends again but there was never a chance of anything more happening between them. There couldn't be a chance.

Chapter Six

All that Meilan could hear was a distant beeping. Though she tried to open her eyes, there was something heavy weighing them down. It felt like there was an invisible force keeping her blind to the world. She tried to move but found that she couldn't. When she tried again, pain raced through her body. Her heart was beating faster in her chest as she heard the beeping speed up.

She tried to remember something about her life – anything – but there were no memories. None. She couldn't remember who she was or where she was. In her mind, there was nothing but beeping, pain, and the annoying inability to open her eyes. Everything else was blank.

Why am I in pain?

Why can't I open my eyes?

What is that beeping?

Where am I?

"Doctor!" someone yelled in the hazy distance.

The voice belonged to a man and it was rich and deep and somehow familiar, but this only confused Meilan more.

"I think she's waking up!"

I am awake, Meilan thought as she struggled to open her eyes again.

After more attempts and strange words murmured by whoever else was where she was, she opened her eyes. Brilliant white lights blinded her. Meilan blinked a few times, trying to adjust to the light. In a few moments, she was able to stare at the ceiling though her head was pounding.

"Where am I?" Pain radiated through her body. Even speaking hurt. Her throat was scratchy and dry. She tried to sit up, but her body wouldn't obey. "Help me! Where am I?"

"You're alright," the same masculine voice from before answered her. She fell back against her bed, her golden eyes wearily lifting to lock on a pair of dark eyes faintly flecked with grey.

For a second, she thought she'd seen those eyes before, but that was impossible. She didn't know this man. She didn't know anything anymore. Her heart continued to race; her hands clammy as she wiped them on the sheets. Each time that she moved, there were wires and tubes pulling against her skin.

"Who are you?" she asked, her voice gruff and low.

The man's eyes widened as he looked at her, his mouth opening slightly. "What do you mean? I'm Jayden. You know me, Meilan. We've been friends since we were young."

Meilan shook her head. "I'm sorry. I don't know who you are. My name is Meilan? Where am I?"

A doctor entered the room. She was tiny and wrapped in a white coat. "I'm going to need you to move so I can take a look at your wife."

Meilan's eyebrows furrowed. "Wife? I'm married to you?"

The man stuttered for a moment, rubbing the back of his neck. "Something like that," he said.

The woman pushed Jayden to the side and grabbed the

charts at the foot of the bed, glancing over them before moving to check her vitals. After a few moments, the doctor stepped back, the warm smile still on her face.

"Good morning, Meilan. I suppose you have a few questions."

"A few."

"Well, my name is Dr. Moore and I would be happy to answer them for you." She pulled over a little stool and sat beside Meilan's bed. "Now, the first thing that you should know is that I am a brain specialist at Renford Memorial in New York City. The second thing is that you are a very lucky woman. But, before we continue talking, how about you have some of this water?"

The doctor grabbed a glass of water from the table beside the bed. She carefully held it against Meilan's lips, allowing her to drink a few sips before placing the glass back on the table.

"Now, how about we talk about what I think is going on?"

Meilan nodded. Any answers that she could get about who she was and where she was would be welcome. She was confused. Nothing made sense. Her head ached. In fact, her entire body ached. If this doctor could even tell her what had happened, she would be one step closer to finding out who she was and who the man standing in the corner of the room was. Jayden watched her, his eyes narrowed and focused as he crossed his arms over his chest. She watched as he nibbled on his bottom lip and shifted his weight from foot to foot.

"Now, I have a few questions to ask. Can you tell me your name?"

"Meilan."

The doctor scribbled something down on her clipboard. "Alright. Now, what about your last name?"

Meilan swallowed, panic rising in her chest. "I don't know that. I can't remember."

Dr. Moore nodded, the comforting look still on her face. "How about where you were born?"

Meilan shook her head. She didn't remember that either. Dr. Moore went through a series of questions, each more difficult than the last. Meilan couldn't remember what month it was or when she first met the man in the room. There was nothing about her life that she could remember.

Finally, the questions ended and she was whisked away for testing. After being prodded and poked for what seemed like hours, she was returned to her room where the man was still waiting for her.

Jayden stood as Meilan was placed back in her bed. Dr. Moore entered once more and sat back on her stool.

"Alright, we have some things that we need to talk about." Dr. Moore smiled at Meilan, reaching forward to squeeze her hand. "Now, do you want your husband in the room while we talk about your prognosis?"

Meilan looked at Jayden. She thought that if she had a husband, she would remember him. Jayden leaned forward in the chair he sat in, clasping his hands together.

"Yes, he can stay."

"Alright," Dr. Moore said as she crossed one leg over the other. "Now, you survived a horrific plane crash. I'm sure your husband can fill you in on that some more later. What we have to talk about is how the coma has affected your brain. It seems like you are experiencing memory loss but through all of the scans that we looked at, there is no permanent damage that we can see."

"What does that mean?" Jayden asked. "You can clearly see that she doesn't remember anything. How is there no damage if she can't remember her life?"

Meilan had to admit that Jayden had a point. If she couldn't remember anything, didn't that mean that there was some sort of permanent damage? How couldn't there be damage if she didn't remember who she was or anything else about her life? Meilan shook her head, her eyes watering as she stared down at the blanket spread across her lap. The ache in her head was growing.

Meilan looked between the doctor and the man who was supposed to be her husband. "Will I ever be able to remember anything?"

Dr. Moore nodded. "I think that your memory should make a full return but there is no way of knowing how long it will take. There are things that we can do to try and trigger the brain but after being in a coma for that long, it is to be expected that your brain is handling your recovery differently than your body. In order to protect you, your brain shut your body down and put you into a coma."

"How long was I asleep for?" Meilan asked, her voice soft as she glanced around the room. There were flowers decorating the tables and a battered copy of a book sat on the arm of the recliner.

"Weeks," Dr. Moore said. "Most of your physical injuries are nearly healed but there is still more recovery left. However, we should be ready to discharge you from the hospital in a few days."

"A few days?" Meilan didn't know how she was supposed to go through her life without remembering who she was. Was the doctor really going to release her to the man that was calling himself her husband? *He had to have given them some kind of proof, right? He can't just take me out of here.*

"Yes. We are going to keep you hear for a few more days while we monitor you. After that, we should be good to release you into the care of your husband." Dr. Moore stood up and offered another smile. "I have to see my next patient now but if you need me or have any more questions, please ask one of the nurses to come get me."

"Thank you," Meilan said as the doctor left.

The room descended into silence as she was left alone with Jayden. She looked over at the man who claimed to be her husband and felt her heart speeding up once again. A blush covered her cheeks as the beeping of the machines sped up along with it.

Jayden was handsome, that much was certain. He had dark eyes and stubble covered his chin. Dark curls were cropped close to his head and there was an easy smile on his face as he looked at her. If she could remember who she was, she was certain that this would be a man she would be more than happy to marry.

"So, you're my husband?" Meilan finally asked as Jayden settled into the recliner and put his feet up on the edge of her bed. She looked at the wrinkles forming in the suit he wore.

"Not exactly. We have known each other a very long time, yes. But we're not married."

"Are we engaged?"

He frowned and shook his head. "No, I'm engaged to another woman. However, the doctors would have kicked me out if I wasn't an immediate relative. I lied to them so they would let me stay with you."

"Do I have a husband then?" Meilan grabbed the bed remote and moved the bed into a seating position. She laced her fingers together and looked at him. "Or a wife?"

Jayden frowned, his eyebrows furrowing and a sad look came across his face. "To be honest, I don't know. You and I haven't talked to each other in well over a decade."

"Why not?"

He shrugged and looked down at his hands. After a moment, he looked back up but he wouldn't make eye contact with her. "There were a lot of things that were outside of our control and even more hurt feelings on both sides from what I have heard in the last couple days."

"And we never tried to keep in touch once over the last thirteen years?"

"No," Jayden said with a sad smile. "No, we didn't."

Meilan nodded, feeling her heart sink in her chest. How had a relationship with someone she had known for years come to such a distance?

Chapter Seven

"Meilan woke up a couple days ago," Jayden said as he and Emma got ready for work. Since discovering him in Meilan's bed, she had made a point of staying in the home they shared instead of taking off to vacation properties. "She's doing pretty well but she doesn't remember anything that happened."

Emma frowned, looking at Jayden in the mirror. "Are you going back over there today?"

"Yeah, but I should be coming home tonight. I'm taking some work with me though. Apparently, the shareholders don't appreciate the CEO taking time off."

"I can see why," she said, her tone hard as she turned to face him. "Why do you keep going over there?"

Jayden looked at the tears gathering in Emma's eyes and put on a gentle smile. He couldn't blame her for being upset with him, not even a little bit. None of this had been what either of them were expecting a few weeks ago and yet here they were, two fish completely out of water. He couldn't be upset that she was worried about their relationship and what might happen now. Hell, he should be thankful that she had forgiven him for lying to her.

"She is my friend and she needs me right now." He wrapped his arms around Emma's waist and pulled her close. "I appreciate you being so understanding about this. And our wedding is only three weeks away now. After, I am taking you on the best honeymoon of your life."

The frown on her face broke, spreading into a smile. "It better be the only honeymoon I ever have."

He bent to kiss her quickly before standing up and grabbing a bag packed with his work and some books for Meilan. Tucked into another pocket were the letters Kevin had brought back a few days ago. "You got it. I'll see you tonight."

Meilan was sitting up in bed and eating a fruit cup when he walked in. For a moment, he was brought back to their high school days. The lunches that she made both of them always had a fruit cup in them. Jayden don't know why she bothered putting them in the lunch boxes – she could never open her own. There would always be a sad little pout as she pushed the fruit cup across the table and waited for Jayden to open it. Briefly he wondered if she had the nurse open the little cup for her before leaving.

"How are you doing?" Jayden set the bag down and pulled out one of the books. He tossed it onto the bed beside Meilan's foot. "This used to be one of your favorite books in high school."

She abandoned the fruit cup to grab the book. "*Dracula?* It doesn't sound familiar."

"Oh, trust me, you loved it. You would go on rants about how women are portrayed and then ask me to read it to you again once I was done. I think *Dracula* came second only to *Peter Pan.*"

Meilan grinned and leaned back against her pillows, opening the book. "You don't have to stay here with me. I talked to my mom today. She said that we were friends. She got quiet when I said that you were pretending to be my husband though. It feels strange to call someone your mother and not remember who they are."

"I bet," Jayden said, glossing over why her mother would have gone quiet. "She looks a lot like you. Carbon copies almost. And I know that I don't have to stay here but I want to. Much better than sitting in an office."

He gave Meilan a sly smile before powering on his laptop and getting to work. She watched from her hospital bed, peeking over her book every now and then as he spoke to the shareholders. Meilan listened as he spoke. He was confident and sure of himself. There was something attractive about the way he spoke with passion or smiled at her every time their eyes met.

When the call was finally done, he closed the laptop and moved the recliner closer to Meilan. Quickly, he plucked the book from her and closed it.

"I think I know what we are going to do to help solve your memory problem."

Meilan smirked and crossed her arms. "Oh, do we now?"

"You and I are going to do things that we used to do back in the day. It might bring some memories back."

"And how exactly are we going to do that when I don't know what I used to do back then, Jayden?"

Jayden shrugged. "Well to start with, you can call me Jay. You never called Jayden. Second, you don't need to remember because I have this interesting little scrapbook that was found with your luggage."

He reached into his bag and pulled out a little book with a brown cover. Meilan reached for it but he held it away from her.

"I don't think so. You and I are going to create new versions of these memories." Meilan nodded but she was far too quiet for his liking. He tucked the scrapbook away and leaned forward, placing his hand on her thigh and giving it a soft squeeze. "What's going on in that head of yours?"

"What if I never remember?" she whispered.

Jayden frowned, feeling like his heart was being ripped out of his chest as tears rolled down her cheeks. "If you never remember then that is okay too."

"No, it's not," she said, her breath hitching as she buried her face behind her hands. "I can't remember anything about my life. I don't know who I am. It's terrifying."

Jayden don't know what compelled him to get out of the chair but before he knew it, he was climbing out of the recliner and into the bed beside her. He wrapped his arms around her, pulling her close.

"I know," he whispered, his lips against her hair as she nestled herself closer to him. The sweet scent of honey and peonies wafted upward. One of the nurses had helped her in the shower recently. "I know that none of this is easy for you but it's going to be okay. We will figure all of this out, alright?"

"You don't know that." Her shoulders rocked with sobs as he held her tighter. Jayden could count the number of times he had seen Meilan cry on a single hand. "For all you know, we are going to spend another couple hours just sitting here and feeling sorry for ourselves and then you are going to remember everything."

"You make that sound like it's a bad thing," she said with a sniffle. "You don't know that for sure."

"There are very few things I am certain about in life. One of those things is that you will get your memory back but until then, you can cry and I will be right here waiting until you're okay again."

Jayden settled back against the pillows, crossing one leg over another and holding Meilan while she sobbed. With each new strangled sound, he felt the tear is his heart widen a little more.

Tears brimmed in his own eyes as he listened to the sound of a woman who may have lost her entire life as it was. His best friend was hurting and there was nothing he could do to fix it.

Instead, he held her tighter and whispered platitudes in her ear. One day they would be okay again but today was not the day.

Chapter Eight

J*ay,*
  I'm sorry that I couldn't tell you that we had to move. I still don't know why we had to move. I tried to tell you a thousand times but the words never came. That was the selfish part of me, I guess. I owe you so much but I couldn't even tell you that I had to leave.

  In fact, there are a lot of things that I never told you. I still don't think I can tell you but maybe one day I will be able to.

Jay,
  California is strange. I wish you were here. You would make everything better. I tried to convince my mother that we should take you with us but it was no use. For some reason, I think that she wanted us apart. I don't know why but I just get this bad feeling, you know?

  Anyway, why didn't you respond to my last letter? I know you're angry, Jay, but I need to talk to you.

Ronald Hansen

* * *

Jay,

Dad is sick and it has me thinking about all the things that we should be doing with our time that we aren't. Have you ever really considered how much time is wasted? There are days where I was mad at him and refused to speak to him for moving us across the country. I would take all of that back now. What if he doesn't make it through?

Of course, his doctor says that the kind of cancer he has isn't that serious. That there is a chance that he will survive. Can you imagine that? A cancer that isn't that bad. It seems impossible and yet, apparently people are entering remission every day.

But yeah. His diagnosis has me thinking about all the time we waste. All the things that we should have said to people while they were alive. It has me thinking that there are things I regret about our friendship. Things that I never told you. I suppose that there is no time like the present, even if you aren't answering my letters. I'm not surprised that you are still angry with me. I would be too if I were you. What I did was entirely unforgivable, though I am selfish enough to wish that you would forgive me.

If you were here right now, you would be telling me to get to the point.

That's something you never understood. Getting to the point is difficult. Being vulnerable is hard as hell. You are so blunt and brave. I suppose you would have to be, growing up the way that you did. Sometimes I wished that our personalities were more alike.

You're probably reading this and cursing me out for not getting to the point. That thought makes me smile. I hope you've learned not to run your mouth since I've been gone these past few months.

The point, Jay, is that I love you.

First Love Never Dies

I had thousands of chances to say that while I lived in New York and I never did. But it's true. I love you.

* * *

Jay,

 It's been months since I sent my last year. A year and a half since I wrote the first. In that last letter, I said that I loved you. I do still. But I can see that you are not going to forgive me anytime soon. That's alright. I'll be in California if you ever want to look me up later in life. Dad is in remission now; in case you care.

 I think that this will be the last time that I write you. It's too painful to sit here and wonder what could have been if you had the same feelings for me that I had for you. It's clear that you don't. Believe me, if nothing else, that much is perfectly clear.

 I don't know if I'll ever get over you but I hope I do.

 Loving you hurts too much.

Chapter Nine

J ayden looked at the tear stains that marred the ink on the page. The letters had been sealed when he had received them. The stains were Meilan's tears. He carefully folded the last letter and slipped it back inside the envelope. The only sound that he could hear was Emma's gentle snores in the other room.

His heart hung heavy in his chest as he hid the letters in the back of a drawer in the closet. Jayden sat in the bench in the center of the walk-in closet, his elbows resting on his knees as he leaned forward. His breathing was shallow and his heart pounded in his chest. Thoughts of all that could have been were swirling around in his mind until they became a mess of emotion.

After a few more minutes, Jayden left the closet and crawled back into bed beside Emma. His fiancée was his future now. Not the woman who had torn out his heart and couldn't remember doing so.

When Jayden arrived at the hospital, Meilan was eagerly waiting. His heart still hung heavy in his chest with the revelations those letters had brought. Jayden knew he couldn't let her see that though. She didn't remember any of what had happened between them. As much as he wanted to yell, wanted to tell her that he had loved her back then too, it was pointless.

Until she smiled at him and the sunlight streaming in the window caught her honey-colored eyes just right. In those moments he was falling for her all over again and he hated himself for it. He had a fiancée. There should be no affectionate feelings beyond friendship between him and Meilan.

Yet, as he stood by her side and looked down at the cast that had been removed, he knew that what he was feeling was more than friendship. Jayden would do whatever it took to stomp out that feeling. They were only friends and Emma was his future.

"I wasn't sure you'd be coming today," she said with a faint laugh. "I know your wedding is in a few days. How is Emma?"

"You know how Emma is. The closer we get to the wedding, the more upset she is. Which only upsets everyone around her."

Meilan grinned. "Well, it is her special day, after all. She is a lucky woman."

Jayden faltered for a moment, unsure of what to say next. It wasn't the reaction he had hoped for from Meilan, if he was being honest. He had wanted something to click in her mind, a memory of the feelings she once had to resurface, as selfish a wish as that was. He was marrying Emma because it felt like the proper thing to do. He had made a promise to her, to love her forever and stand by her side. The wedding – as much as he had never wanted it – was the way Emma saw that promise as being upheld. He had known since the beginning of their relationship that he would do what it took to keep her happy. Lately though neither of them had been happy; a realization that haunted him.

It's better this way, he thought as he looked at her. *She doesn't feel that way about you anymore. You don't feel that way about her. You are getting married and that is all there is to the story.*

"What's new with you?"

"Nothing really." Meilan continued to smile, but it faltered briefly.

"Are you alright? Did the doctor say something?" Jayden asked.

Meilan's eyes welled with tears. "Yeah. Dr. Moore did visit. And it's good news."

"Then why are you crying?"

Meilan laughed and wiped away the tears that fell. "I don't know. I'm being released from the hospital but I don't remember anything. I've been talking to my mother but she thinks that it is best if I stay in New York right now. She thinks that your ideas of acting out childhood memories will help. And then we talked to the doctors together. They said that the brain is a temperamental thing and there is no one way to trigger the return of my memories. But Dr. Moore said that the memories I have can be triggered by experiencing some of the same things. Something about sensory memory but I didn't fully understand what she was talking about after that."

"You have somewhere to go," Jayden said before he could think it over further. Emma would forgive him. At least, he hoped that she would. "I have a couple of extra properties in the city. There's one really nice home in the Hamptons that you could stay at."

"Are you sure that Emma won't mind?"

"Absolutely not," he said with confidence. *Emma is going to kill you.*

There was no way that Emma would be okay with a woman she already viewed as a threat staying in one of their homes. There would be a massive fight, he could already see it coming. He knew it. However, he wasn't about to just toss Meilan onto the streets or put her into a hotel when she was still missing her memory. She needed a place where at least one familiar face could be close by when needed.

"I don't want to be an inconvenience to anyone." Meilan smiled at him softly as she twisted the blanket that lay across her legs. "I feel like there was a reason that I was supposed to come to New York. Does that sound silly?"

"Not even a little bit," Jayden said as he started moving around the room and packing up the few belongings Meilan had. "If you think you're supposed to be here then here is where you will stay. I have more than enough properties to allow you to stay at one until you decide what you want to do."

"I feel like I am asking for too much. I don't even really know you anymore."

"It's fine," Jayden said, pausing to grin at her. "I would be happy to offer you a place to stay. You need more time to recover and I have big plans for helping you remember everything. It's much easier to do if you're in the state."

Liar, his mind screamed at him as he packed up the few sets of clothing that Emma had bought Meilan. *You only want her around to see if those old feelings are still there.*

Chapter Ten

Meilan stared at the giant white house, the balcony overlooking the driveway. The wrought iron gates swung open and Jayden drove in. There were black shutters around the windows and giant hedges trimmed to perfection. Emerald green grass was on either side of the drive way and Meilan was certain that someone had taken the time to make sure that every single blade of grass was the same height. There was no way that the level of perfection that was the yard could be archived without that kind of dedication.

"You own this place?" Meilan asked as she stared at the windows that took up most of the walls. The entire first floor looked like it was mainly glass with a little bit of giant white stone showing.

"Yeah," Jayden said, his cheeks taking on a pink hue as he drove up the winding road. He rubbed the back of his neck and looked at Meilan. "It's a little bit excessive but I like coming up here and spending most of my summer here."

"I can see why," Meilan said, looking at the walkway that ran high above the ground, connecting the main house to a smaller building. "You could make a lot of money if you sold this place. How much is it worth?"

Jayden's blush deepened as he stopped the car by the steps that led to the front door. "I already make a ton of money. And I don't know how much the house cost. That sounds horrible, doesn't it?"

"It sounds like you have more money than you know what to do with."

"You're not wrong," he said as he got out of the car. "Now, let's get your bags inside and give you a tour of the place."

"I'm sure you have better things to do," Meilan said, getting out of the car and walking up the stairs to the front door. "Your wedding is in two days. Aren't you supposed to be running around and going through all of the last-minute details?"

Jayden chuckled and unlocked the door, letting them inside. "No. Trust me, Emma wants me nowhere near the wedding. In fact, the farther away I am, the happier that she is."

"That's horrible. It's your wedding too."

Jayden shrugged before heading to the car to get Meilan's bags. When he came back inside, she was wandering through the kitchen and examining the marble countertops. If Jayden were being honest, the house looked like a show home. He had an interior designer decorate it; he couldn't be bothered. It was only the home he escaped to for the summer. However, looking at Meilan pacing across the hardwood floors, her nose wrinkling in distaste like she used to do when they were younger, he had the desire to change everything impersonal in his home. He would change everything she didn't like to make her happy. To keep her in New York with him.

He shook the thoughts from his head and removed his beeping phone from his pocket. "Alright," Jayden said with a sigh. "I have to go back to the city for the evening. It seems like there is a problem with the venue. Will you be alright on your own?"

Meilan looked at him and nodded. "I think I remember how to make a sandwich."

He paled. "If you need help, I can stay. It's okay."

Meilan laughed, the sound light and airy as she shook her head. "Don't worry. That was a joke. I still remember how to do basic things but all of my personal memories are gone."

"You had me worried there for a moment."

"I know. Don't worry about me though. You've already done more than I could have ever hoped for. Thank you."

"Don't thank me. You would do the same for me if our roles were reversed."

"I don't know that I would though."

Jayden shrugged as he walked out the front door and onto the porch. "I know that you would. If you need anything, I programmed my number into the cell phone I gave you a couple days ago."

"I'll be fine," Meilan said as she walked to the door and took the keys from him. "If I need anything, I'll let you know. Try to enjoy your wedding."

Jayden smiled, his heart aching in his chest. He hated hearing those words coming from her mouth. In a perfect world, she never would have moved away and they would have spent the rest of their lives together. Now, he was walking toward a future with another woman. Yes, he loved Emma. He wanted to spend the rest of his life with Emma. At least, he thought that he did.

Jayden shook the thoughts from his mind before giving Meilan a soft smile. "I'll see you after the honeymoon, okay? Think you can survive two weeks without me?"

First Love Never Dies

Meilan chucked. "If what you've told me has happened, I've survived years without you."

Though he knew that she didn't mean the words as malicious, they still cut deep.

Chapter Eleven

Normally, Jayden would spend his lunch break hunched over his desk and peering at a series of reports. He would read until the letters and numbers blurred in front of him. Halfway through lunch, Emma would normally call and complain about her day. He would spend the rest of his lunch pacifying her and ignoring his secretary who would try to mime hanging up the phone. Sometimes, on the extra special days, he would talk with his doctors about the state of his kidneys and alternatives to organ transplants.

Today, Jayden was walking through the little shops downtown and looking for a gift for Meilan. He wasn't sure why the sudden urge to buy her something had overcome him but it had. The moment his alarm went off, signaling lunchtime, he was out of his office and heading to the shops.

After what seemed like countless hours spent window shopping – though he checked his phone and it had only been twenty minutes – he found a tiny boutique with stunning dresses in the window. They were soft and understated, the kind of thing that Emma would hate but Meilan would absolutely love. He browsed through the shop, the scent of vanilla and baked goods thick in the air though he couldn't see any candles burning.

Meilan would look beautiful in this, he thought as he ran his fingers along the pleated silk of an emerald green dress. In the back of his mind there was a voice telling him that this was wrong. That looking for a dress for another woman could be perceived as something *wrong.* He knew that Emma would be upset if she knew but he couldn't bring himself to care.

The green dress wasn't right. It wouldn't fall in the right way. Meilan had always liked clothing more fitted than baggy – at least she used to. He wasn't sure if she still did.

"Can I help you with anything?" a woman asked, appearing from behind a rack of blue dresses.

"That obvious?" Jayden said, a chuckle following his words. The woman smiled and shrugged.

"You said it. Not me."

He nodded, glancing around the store again. "I think that I'll be okay."

She nodded. "Let me know if you need anything."

He offered her another smile before moving deeper into the little shop. Everything was too bright and frilly. Meilan had never been that kind of girl when they were in high school. She liked the simple, classic look. Something that would scream elegance and class.

That was when he saw the perfect dress. Well, he thought that it might be the perfect dress. It was hard to see through the cloud of rhinestones from dresses on either side of the one he was eyeing. Jayden weaved through the racks of dresses until he reached his destination.

The fabric was soft and silky as he held it out. The black fabric shone softly under the lights, a light sheen tracing the draped neckline. Two tiny straps held it on the hanger and he could see where the fabric was sliced high along one side.

Perfect, he thought.

When Meilan woke up late that afternoon, there was a large white box sitting on the plush ottoman at the end of her bed. She sat up, stretching and smoothing down her hair. She ran her fingers through the knots, eyeing the package. It could only have been from Jayden but she didn't know what he would buy for her that he hadn't bought already with money her mother had sent. Though, she suspected that he was using more than just the money her mother had sent.

"What are you?" Meilan whispered as she crawled to the edge of the bed and grabbed the box off of the ottoman.

She carefully undid the black silk ribbon from its bow, enjoying the smooth feeling over her fingertips. When she lifted the box lid, pale pink tissue paper was waiting to be unwrapped. Meilan's heart was beating faster. This didn't seem like the kind of present that one friend would get another.

Once the tissue paper was tossed to the side, she pulled out the dress. Immediately, tears sprung to her eyes. It looked nicer than anything she had seen in the recent weeks. It was a much nicer dress than the hospital gown she had last been wearing.

Careful to avoid injuring herself more, she got up and walked across the room to the giant mirror. She stood in front of it, holding the dress against her body as tears flowed down her cheeks.

The dress was beautiful and it was definitely not the kind of present she thought a friend would buy another one. With a smile, Meilan held the dress close to her body, swaying to the imaginary music in her mind.

Chapter Twelve

W hen Jayden got home, Emma was in tears and her mother was sitting by the front door with a frown on her face and a phone pressed against her ear. Jayden dropped his keys in the little bowl on the table and crossed the foyer, pulling his fiancée off of the floor.

"What's wrong?" he asked as he wrapped his arms around her waist and kissed her hair. "Hey, no more tears. What's going on with the venue? How can I help?"

"You can't help," Emma said between sobs. "The entire wedding is going to be ruined now."

"Slow down, breathe, and then tell me what you're talking about. You've had this place booked since the day after we got engaged so what is going on?"

"The kitchen burned down."

"That's not so bad."

Jayden regretted his words the moment they were out of his mouth. Emma pulled back, her eyes narrowing as she glared at him. She shoved his arms away from her and the tears dried, replaced with what he could only assume was pure fury.

Jayden stepped away, raising his hands in a sign of defense as Emma passed back and forth. Several times her mouth opened but no sound came out. He could feel the tension in the room rising as he stepped back more, trying to put distance between them in case she snapped and came flying at him. Emma was never abusive but he didn't know what a white-hot rage about the cancellation of their wedding venue would do to her. It was safer to be as far away as possible.

"That's not so bad?" Emma's voice was high-pitched. Her mother shot her a glare. "Don't look at me like that mother. I'm allowed to be upset when my entire wedding is ruined. What are we even supposed to do now? We have nowhere to get married!"

"We could always just go down to the courthouse," Jayden said with a small smile that he hoped she would see as a joke. Instead of improving the situation, it only made matters worse. The tears started all over again.

"Are you kidding me? We have hundreds of guests coming. We can't get married in a disgusting courthouse."

"Honey," he said softly, wiping away her tears before kissing her forehead. "We are going to figure this out, okay? We have that home in the Hamptons. It has more than enough room in the backyard to have a wedding."

Emma paused for a minute, blinking slowly as she looked at him. "You know, that might work. I hadn't considered that before but outdoor weddings are all the rage. Especially when you have a backyard like ours. We could get married in the big gazebo that's there by the barn."

"We could get everything that you want set up. The caterers could use the kitchen in the main house and all of the guests could use the barn or guest house washroom. We could get the handyman to build a dancefloor by the pool."

Emma grinned and wrapped her arms around Jayden. "You

are a brilliant man. I am going to start calling around and see what I can get done. Will you make sure that mother gets home? I don't want her in the way and trying to change the new vision for the wedding. You know if it's up to her we would have to get married at that stuffy country club."

Jayden smiled. "I think I can do that."

Emma took off to go plan the changes to their wedding. Jayden sighed and leaned against the wall, tilting his head back to look at the ceiling. There was an uneasy feeling in his chest as he thought of bringing the wedding to Meilan. It was a cruel thing to do; marry the woman you love while the woman you used to love would be watching from the window.

"We can even throw a party tomorrow night," Emma's mother said with a smile as she looked at Jayden, her eyes narrowing. "Maybe make up for all of the sneaking around that you have been doing the last couple of weeks.

Jayden nodded, a hollow feeling in his chest. "Sounds like a good idea."

There was classical music coming from the string quartet set up by the pool. Jayden had told Meilan about the party only hours earlier and sent one of his assistants over with a dress. He couldn't blame her if she didn't want to come to the party though. If he were her and had just gone through what she went through, he would want nothing to do with a party.

Jayden had a glass of champagne in his hand and was standing under a canopy of lights with his other arm around Emma's waist. She was laughing as she spoke to one of his shareholders. He could see the dollar signs in the man's eyes, knowing that Emma would only be an asset to all future business meetings. She could charm the bark off a tree with the blink of an eye.

In that moment, while Jayden was starting to enjoy himself, he heard conversations stop. Most were still going, dying down one-by-one until there was nothing but the sound of the quartet. Jayden looked around, wondering what could have caused the sudden silence.

It was then that he saw her.

Meilan was gliding across the stone patio, her hair falling in soft waves down her back. He could see the toes of her bare feet with each step, her body still too injured for heels. A black dress clung to her body, held up by straps barely bigger than a piece of string. The neckline was draped in soft folds. A long slit traced its way up her left leg with each step. Her soft smile was visible for all as several people approached her.

"I thought you said that she wouldn't be coming to this tonight," Emma said, her nails digging into Jayden's arm. He tore his eyes away from Meilan and looked down at Emma. "I thought that you said she would be staying in her room and wouldn't have anything to do with my wedding."

Jayden sighed, not wanting to get into this again. "I thought that she would be staying in her room tonight. Of course, I would have told you that she was going to be coming to the party if I thought that she was."

"Where did she even get that dress?"

Jayden paled, knowing that he was about to admit what Emma would deem a deadly and likely unforgivable mistake. "I had my assistant bring one over in case she did decide to come to the party."

Emma scoffed and plastered on a fake smile as people passed by. As soon as they were out of earshot, she released Jayden's arm and stepped back. "You have got to be kidding me. You have not only given her a place to live, paid her medical bills, and who knows what else, but now you are giving her permission to come to my wedding? Are you kidding me, Jayden? How could you do this to me?"

"Do this to you?" His voice rose, his steady control on his temper giving way. He could feel the eyes on him as people turned to watch but he didn't care. "What are you even going on about? So, what if she came to the party? Why does it matter if she is living here while she recovers?"

"I look like an idiot who can't hold on to her man," Emma said, her voice low and dangerous as she stepped toward him. Under the canopy of lights, he could see the glimmer in her eyes as tears threatened to fall. "I love you and this looks like you are parading your affair around. If you are having one with her, it ends now. Do you hear me?"

Jayden gaped at her before stepping forward and pulling Emma into a tight hug. "I am not having an affair. I promise. I love you and I never want you to think that I could do something like that to you, okay?"

Emma sniffed and stepped away, wiping the tears from her cheeks. "I need to go clean up. I'll be back in a few moments, okay?"

"Call me if you need anything."

Emma nodded and walked away. Jayden turned, searching the crowd once more for Meilan. After a couple of minutes and a circle around the dance floor, he saw her standing on a man's shoes as he spun her around and around the floor. Meilan's smile was wide and genuine, her laughter rising above the sound of the music. She clung to the man as he spun her in rapid circles, moving her around all of the other couples while they were completely lost in their own little world.

Jayden's world became green with envy as he wished he could be in that world.

In the two days leading up to the wedding, Jayden didn't sleep. Most of his nights were spent tossing and turning, nightmares running through his mind in the few hours he could get any sleep at all. Thoughts of Meilan and all that could have been were constant reminders of everything that he was losing. Jayden tried to think of all that he was gaining with Emma by his side but his heart and mind continued to argue.

He spent most of the days leading up to the wedding going back and forth in his mind. Jayden knew that he loved Emma – at least part of him did – but when did loving someone stop being enough for him?

Looking at the picture of her that had been his phone's background, he sighed and leaned back against the door frame. There was no passion. They didn't have fun together anymore. She wasn't the person that had sat beside him in the hospital anymore. The sweet girl who had sat beside him with tears in her eyes, threatening the doctors and promising to never leave. Now, she was the woman pursuing a career and a life that was independent from him. He didn't have a problem with that. No person should be completely reliant on another but without his healthcare in the way, there wasn't much forcing them together. There wasn't much that left them wanting to spend time with each other. They had work, friend groups that never got along, and different interests.

Still, he looked at her and he was sure he loved her. What he wasn't sure of was if he felt that love. If there wasn't something more that was supposed to be there.

And then there was Meilan.

When he looked at her, there was something inside that warmed him to the core. He would – *he had* – dropped his entire life to be with her. If he was given the chance, he knew that he would do it again. There were many things he regretted in his lifetime but most of them had to do with letting Meilan go all of those years ago.

"I'm screwed," he whispered to himself as he left the door frame and made his way to the stairs. It would be time to get married soon. As much as he had his doubts, he had made Emma a promise.

Jayden stood in front of the back doors in the main house, looking out over the backyard where all of the guests were starting to arrive. Emma and her bridesmaid were getting ready in the guesthouse. Once they were ready, Jayden would have to meet Emma up on the catwalk for their first look.

His hands shook as he tried to tie the navy-blue tie that hung loose around his neck. Turning away from the door, he saw Meilan in a doorway. His heart betrayed him, hammering away in his chest though his decision was already made. Jayden's palms were sweaty as he gripped the tie tighter and tried once more to get it into a respectable knot. It was an impossible task with the way his hands shook and the honey-colored eyes that were fixated on him.

"You look nice," she said with a soft smile. "Are you excited?"

Jayden shrugged and gave up his attempt with the tie. There was no way that he could get his hands to stay still long enough to make a proper knot. Excited was an emotion but it certainly wasn't the one that he was feeling. Especially not after the other night.

"Yeah, I guess you could call it that."

Meilan cocked an eyebrow and crossed her arms. "You are marrying the love of your life. You should sound far more excited than that."

"What if she isn't the love of my life?" he said, his voice sounding hollow as he looked at Meilan. He wasn't sure where that had come from but it seemed to be the only clear thing he had thought in days. "What if Emma isn't the love of my life? What if there is another person out there waiting for me and neither of us know it yet?"

Meilan dropped her arms and walked across the room, reaching for his tie. "You love her, don't you?"

"Yeah."

"So, how do you know that she isn't the person that is meant for you?" Meilan's hands working quickly, knotting the tie neatly before tightening it. "How do you know right this minute that she isn't the one for you?"

Jayden looked down at Meilan, the beautiful honey-colored eyes staring up at him. He could smell peonies and honey in her shampoo and he loved the way a tinge of pink coated her cheeks. His heart hammered in his chest as he stared at her, all of the old feelings he once had for her flooding back. In that moment, he wanted to take her away from the wedding and find a corner to hide in. Their conversation was long overdue.

"I just know," he said softly as Meilan's hands dropped from his tie.

Meilan nodded, the pink in her cheeks growing darker as she looked away from him. "Look, I don't know what the relationship between you two is like. But I know that I wouldn't want to marry a man who is having second thoughts. If I was going to marry you, I would want to know that you are really in it for better or worse."

"I couldn't have picked a worse time to have my doubts," he said with a wry smile. "The last few weeks have thrown a major wrench in the way that I thought my life was going. What I once was certain about now seems to be this tangled mess in my head."

Meilan nodded. "I understand that."

Jayden sighed and looked back out at the wedding once more. "I don't know if I can go through with this. How can I marry somebody when I don't know that they are the one?"

"What if you have more than one person that can be the one?"

Jayden wanted to yell at her, to remind her that she was his first love. He wanted to put it all on the table and talk about everything that they had ever gone through together. In his mind, there was an unfinished relationship with her – one that she didn't remember no matter how desperately he wanted her to. The words in the letters bounced around in his mind. She had loved him back then but did she still love him now?

Getting married without knowing the answer seemed wrong but the Meilan standing before him couldn't give him an answer. She didn't remember enough of what was going on to tell him how she felt. That was perhaps the worst part of what he was feeling in that moment. Even if he had a chance with her, right now they would be starting from the beginning.

Finally, he sighed and looked at her. "You're right. I guess I'm just having cold feet."

"From what the wedding shows on the television have told me, that is completely normal." Meilan smiled and reached out to smooth his tie. "You'll be happy once the ceremony is over."

Jayden looked at Meilan, wishing that recognition would spark in her gaze. "I'm sure you're right. Thank you for being such a good friend."

Meilan grinned wider and butterflies erupted in his stomach. "Anytime. It's the least that I can do after all you have done for me."

He looked at the clock on the wall. "I have to go meet Emma now. You know, you can come to the wedding if you want."

"I'll watch from the balcony in my room. I wouldn't want to intrude on your special day." Meilan stepped back and nodded. "You're good to go."

He watched as she turned and walked away. Everything in him wanted to stop her. To tell her that it wasn't intruding when she was the one that was meant to be beside him at that altar.

None of it would matter though. She didn't remember him – *them* – and he had already promised himself to another.

Jayden did what any good man would. He turned and walked up the stairs to the catwalk, saying one final goodbye to the girl that he had once loved and to the one he had promised to love for the rest of his life. As he walked, he tried to ignore that feeling of his heart shattering the same way it had the day he found out that Meilan had disappeared.

Chapter Thirteen

Emma walked down the catwalk looking more beautiful than ever. Jayden met her in the middle, a smile on his face as he looked down at the woman he was going to marry. This was supposed to be the happiest moment of his life. Looking at her should have been enough to make his whole heart skip a beat. It should have been the cementing moment in – well – everything.

Every doubt he'd had should have been washed away. The rising moment. He should have been shaking with the anticipation. But instead, there was just... a dull sort of knowing. The smile slowly dropped from his face. Their eyes met.

Emma smiled at him, and he wanted so badly to return the smile; to feel the same way she was clearly feeling. But instead, there was a hollowness in his chest, something that daunted him. Dread, cold and uneasy, formed a lump in his throat that was hard to swallow past.

He struggled, his lips twitching as he looked at her. There was no warm and fuzzy feeling as he looked at her. Nothing like when he looked at Meilan.

There was no denying that Emma looked amazing. No denial at all. He knew that he could spend the rest of his life by her side. They would be a dynamic power couple with well-paid careers and bright futures. Eventually, they would settle down in a brownstone outside of the city and have two kids – one boy and one girl. Looking at Emma, he could see it all before him even if it felt wrong.

They could really make something of their future.

But.

That was the problem.

He thought about his future with her, and it made the ugly *but* rear up, like a cobra, crown extended, getting ready to strike. He breathed in hard, trying to settle what he was feeling, but it didn't help.

This wasn't going to work.

Right then, Jayden could see that. And yet, today was supposed to be amazing. It was a highlight for Emma, something she had been looking forward to for a long while.

You promised to love her forever, the voice in the back of his mind whispered. He plastered on a smile. It felt wrong to bring this up now. *I won't ruin this day for her.*

And yet, the longer he stood there, the more cracks he could feel starting to fracture the veneer. Jayden wasn't sure how long he could keep it together, now that he had realized he didn't love Emma: not the way he was supposed to.

"Say something," Emma said with a smile as their photographer worked around them. Jayden grabbed her hands and brought them to his lips, placing a kiss across her knuckles.

"You look amazing," he said softly before dropping one hand and giving her a small twirl beneath his arm. Emma laughed and grinned up at him. "More beautiful than the day we met if that's possible."

Wrong, his mind screamed as he looked down at the honey-colored eyes staring up at him. The color was right but everything else was wrong. This was not the girl that had made sure he was eating. It was not the girl who set him up for the success he found. Emma was not the person he had taught English. They hadn't spent part of their high school years together. She didn't know the person he used to be or the person that he was now. She only saw the Jayden that she wanted to see.

And it was wrong, like a car crash playing out in slow motion. The tires screeched. The metal crunched like a thunder clap. There was a leak in the oil, and flames were about to ignite.

This was wrong.

Being with her was wrong.

How could Jayden have ever thought this was the right choice?

It was too much. He couldn't keep the fake smile plastered into place. It fell away, crumbling at the edges. The tension pulled tight through his brows until it was impossible to miss how uneasy he felt.

"What's wrong?" Emma asked, her hands coming up to cup his face. Her thumbs smoothed over the wrinkles caused by his frown. "This is our special day. You should be happy."

"It's not that," Jayden said as he looked down at her. He cupped her hands, turning his head to kiss her palm before lowering both of their hands. "You and I don't know each other anymore."

As soon as he said it, he knew that the words were true.

That was the problem. He didn't know Emma. And she didn't know him, either.

It was a loaded statement. The gun cocked, aimed, and the trigger pulled. He could see the moment Emma realized what he was implying, how all of her poise seemed to fade until she was left raw and open, like a picked-at wound.

Her eyes started to glisten as she took a stumbling step back.

The photographer lowered the camera. Jayden could feel all eyes on him from the bridesmaids standing in the doorway. They had heard him, and while they might not have known all the gritty details, they knew things were about to come ripping apart at the seams.

One of them whispered, "Did I hear that right?"

Another replied, "No way. There's no way he could be pulling this now, of all times. It's just pre-ceremony jitters. My uncle got them too, but they worked it out."

Emma turned around to glare at her friends, and within a moment all of them scattered. Jayden could hear the photographer making excuses as she stepped away, giving the couple space.

They were wrong, of course. These weren't just jitters. This was something that had been building for a long time, but that he had only just realized. The timing wasn't good. He could admit that much.

But the timing didn't change the way Jayden felt.

"We're about to go down and get married," Emma said, her voice thick with the lump forming in her throat. She blinked hard, trying to prevent tears from spilling over before they could ruin her carefully applied makeup. "What are you talking about, Jayden?"

Jayden fumbled for a moment, trying to find the right words. "You and I have never really known each other. We're about to spend the rest of our lives together, but we don't know the first thing about each other."

"That's not true," Emma argued. "We know each other. We love each other. That's why we're here today!"

Jayden frowned, trying to find a better way to explain it. Maybe if he picked his words carefully enough, said them kindly enough, it would take away some of the sting. He told her, "We've become strangers lately. Or maybe there was a part of us that always were. Yes, you've been by me for the kidney infection and the biggest moments of my career. We watch movies together and go to parties but there has to be more than that. We have to *know* each other."

Emma shook her head. "I don't understand what you're saying. Of course we know each other. You are being ridiculous." There was a crack in her voice. She sounded seconds away from full-out crying. "If we didn't know each other, we wouldn't be here!"

Jayden couldn't keep the frustration out of his own tone when he told her, "No, we don't know each other. We really don't."

"You're saying all of this because of that woman, aren't you?" Emma stared at him with wide eyes, the hurt clear. She took a step backwards, as if she was about to bolt. "You're saying all this because she's more than a friend to you."

Jayden sighed and linked his hands behind his neck, pacing back and forth. "This has very little to do with Meilan. You know that you and I have been at odds with each other for a long time. We have nothing in common anymore and it is not fair to either of us to keep going on this way."

And that was when the ice broke, swallowing both of them.

With very little room left to deny what was happening, Emma let out a shoulder-shaking sob. Her hand flew up, pressing against her mouth like she might be able to force the sound back inside. Now the tears were impossible to hold back, spilling down her cheeks in rivulets, smearing her carefully applied black eyeliner in the process.

"You want to break up on the day of my wedding? Are you kidding me, Jayden? You couldn't have thought this through before? I thought that we loved each other. I thought that we were going to spend the rest of our lives together and now you are telling me that you don't want any part of that?"

He looked at Emma, his vision becoming blurry as he watched the tears roll down her face. "I'm sorry. It's—"

But she shook her head, taking another step backwards. Her heel gave a loud, echoing click against the tile. There was venom in her voice when she spat out, "Don't you dare say that. Don't you dare! After all you've done, you're about to give me the line about still being friends? I don't think so."

"I'm sorry," Jayden said, reaching for her. She stepped out of his reach, her hands curling into fists at her side. "I really do love you but I can't marry you."

"You can stand in front of everyone we know and tell them that then," Emma said, her voice cold as she wiped the tears from beneath her eyes. Despite the fact that she was keeping her voice steady, her hands still showed undeniable trembling. Her fingers tried to wipe away the tears, but they just smeared her make up that much more. "I thought we were going to be together forever. I wanted to grow old with you. I thought we were perfect together."

Jayden sighed. "You never thought that, Emma. You can't tell me that you haven't wondered if we were really supposed to be together or not."

"I really did think that," Emma insisted. "If I hadn't, I never would have agreed to marry you. And if you didn't think it…" She paused, pulling in a breath to stabilize her voice. When she spoke next, the words cut through the air like a knife. "If you didn't think it, you should have told me before today."

She turned on her heel and fled the catwalk. Jayden sighed and looked out over the edge at his guests. Breaking the news to them was going to lead to a lot of questions that he didn't want to answer. Emma's family would hate them for the rest of their lives and there was a good chance he just made an enemy out of some of his business partners.

He raked a hand through his hair, trying to remind himself

the breakup was worth it. He would rather have a rough, embarrassing moment now than a future married to someone he didn't love; a future where everything would be daunting and hard to work through.

Still, he had to brace himself for it. Already, he could imagine how poorly it would go. How Emma's mother would react to the news.

After a few more moments, Jayden walked into the backyard, ready to tell everybody that he had changed his mind. He owed Emma at least that much. Since he was the one who had called an end to their future, he would be the one to stand in front of dozens of people – their families, their friends, their coworkers – and tell them all that he had broken off their engagement on the day they were going to get married.

Here goes nothing, he thought as he walked down the aisle, heads turning to him and whispers starting.

Chapter Fourteen

"That didn't look like it was fun," Meilan said the next morning when Jayden came down the stairs. "How are you holding up?"

Jayden groaned and headed into the kitchen, making a beeline for the pot of coffee. "I don't want to talk about that right now."

Meilan nodded and pulled herself up to sit on the counter. "How about we do something to take your mind off of it then? You wanted to start living out our childhood memories, why don't we do that?"

Jayden looked at her, a small smile spreading across his face though it didn't meet his eyes. "Alright. How about we go to Central Park?"

"I would like that."

"Let me go get dressed and then we will go."

Jayden was quick to down his coffee before going to get dressed. When he returned, Meilan was standing by the door with a travel mug of coffee in her hand. He smiled, memories of early mornings at school flooding back to him. She had rarely been spotted in the halls of their high school without coffee. More than once she had called it her life force.

When they got to the park, Meilan headed straight for a sunny spot out of reach of the shadows. She laid down in the grass, her coffee beside her.

"Tell me about your life," Meilan said, glancing at Jayden as he lay down beside her.

"What do you want to know?" He crossed his arms behind his head and stared up at the sky. All of the noises of the city seemed farther away when he was in the park.

"Everything that you have ever told me and then some."

He chuckled. "Well, in case you couldn't tell yet, my mother was white and my father was African American. Mom died in the hospital room shortly after giving birth. Father didn't want me or something like that. I don't know what his story was and nobody else does either. Spent years jumping around from foster home to group home to juvenile detention centers and back again."

Meilan peeked at him from the corner of her eyes. "Where's your father?"

"As of last month or the last twenty and some odd years? I don't really know." Jayden gave a hollow laugh. "I've never really known. I don't know who he is or where he lives. I don't even know why he left us."

"Have you ever thought about reaching out to him? Maybe things happened differently than you thought that they did. Maybe he really did love you but he had to leave. There could have been a lot of things going on in his life and perhaps it was better that he left."

"You always used to say that when we were younger. You made excuses for him where I wouldn't. As I got older, I started to think that maybe you were right. Maybe there were a lot of things going on that I didn't understand about his life."

"And what do you think now?" Meilan asked, staring at the clouds in the sky. "Do you still think that I might have been right?

Jayden shook his head and looked at her. "You and I used to talk about one day finding my father, you know that? I used to be so bitter and resentful back then. You would always insist that one day I would want to find him. You were right. After you left and I finished school, I started looking for him."

"Did you find him?"

"No." Jayden swallowed the lump in his throat. "I only looked for him for a day or two. Nothing that would actually allow me to find him. I think that I just wanted to make myself feel better. Tell myself that I tried to reconnect with him but he just didn't want me in his life."

"So, you gave up without really trying?"

"Yeah. I could have searched harder for him. Hell, I still could. I have more than enough money and if anyone were going to find him, it would be Kevin."

"Do you want to?" Meilan glanced at Kevin. "Now that you have the money, you could probably find him if you really wanted to."

"I don't know," Jayden said. "There is a lot of bad blood there."

Meilan nodded and rolled onto her side, tucking one arm beneath her head to look at him. Jayden copied her position, staring at her and wondered if now was the time to talk about the letters. About whether or not she still loved him. Why she had come to New York in the first place.

Maybe you should tell her that your kidneys may kill you. He shoved the thought to the back of his mind and locked it in a steel box, welding it shut. His intrusive thoughts would not ruin their reunion. He could tell her that he might die later. For now, he wanted to bask in the feeling of being with her again.

"What are you thinking about?" Meilan asked.

Jayden reached out to brush away a strand of hair that was falling into her face. "You're beautiful."

Her cheeks turned a bright pink as she averted her eyes. "You just ended your marriage. Are you sure that's a good idea?"

Jayden rolled his eyes and grinned. "Or maybe, I'm not flirting with you and I'm just stating a fact."

Meilan chuckled. "Nice try. I may not remember you but I do know when somebody is flirting with me. After a few days of being around your gardener, I have learned that much again."

Jealousy flared up. Jayden would have a talk with his gardener when he got back to the Hamptons about what was appropriate behavior and what wasn't.

Jayden and Meilan sat in the sun, talking about everything that they could think of. Jayden talked about all of the things that they had done together while Meilan sat there and listened. She loved listening to him though the life he spoke about was foreign to her.

"You know," Jayden said that night when they arrived back at the house. "I have some letters that belong to you. I think that you should read them. I'll be away for the next week for a business meeting. We can talk about them when I get back."

"Should I be worried about what these letters say?"

"I don't know," Jayden said, looking at the way the moonlight shone across her face as they stood on the porch. "But I think that reading those letters may bring some of your memories back."

"I know why getting my memories back is important to me, but why do you care?"

He studied her for a moment, a sad smile appearing on his face. "You and I were not given a fair shot at a lot of things. I'm not saying that reading those letters will change anything but I am saying that it can't hurt to try."

Chapter Fifteen

O ver the past week, Meilan had read all of her letters dozens of times. She had studied the words on the page over and over again. Each time she read one, she wondered if this was all that she had been feeling at that time. There was nothing that came to her. No memories of Jayden or their lives. Her heart was sinking to her feet fast as the disappointment set in. They had both been hoping that these letters would restore her memories.

Meilan flipped through the letters again, desperate to remember something.

Jayden. Moving across the country to get away from him. It was all there in ink and tear smudges and yet she still couldn't remember it. She was certain that the writing was hers but there was nothing there that made the memories reappear in her mind. It was still all just speculation. Her memories of her life were still as evasive as ever.

Meilan set aside the letters and stood on the balcony that overlooked the driveway. Jayden would be returning back to the Hamptons before she knew it. When he did get back, they would have a lot to talk about. Though she didn't know what was going on with him, he had cancelled his wedding. That had to have something to do with her.

She stood on the balcony for hours, waiting for the sleek black car to come through the iron gates. As the sun was setting, the gates swung open and Jayden pulled into the driveway. Meilan's hands shook as she clutched the edge of the balcony.

Jayden got out of the car, the sleeves of his dress suit rolled up and dark circles beneath his eyes. He tilted his head back, looking at where Meilan stood. Despite his obvious exhaustion, a bright smile spread across his face.

Meilan raced down the stairs, eager to meet Jayden at the door. Even if she didn't remember who he was, she knew that she liked the person she had been spending time with. The front door was opening as Meilan came to a stop at the bottom of the stairs. Jayden dropped his bags to the side and looked at her, a hopeful smile on his face.

With her heart sinking even further than it had before, Meilan shook her head. She couldn't remember anything. Jayden's smile faltered slightly but he kept it in place as he shut the door behind him.

"How has your week been?" he asked as he crossed the foyer to the bottom of the stairs. He pulled Meilan into a hug, lifting her off the bottom step and twirling her around before putting her down. Meilan laughed and looked at him.

"It's been a good week. I can't remember anything though. No matter how many times I read those letters, nothing would come back to me. I'm sorry."

Jayden's smiled dropped as he reached out to ruffle her hair. "Don't be sorry. It's not your fault at all. The plane crash messed with your brain. It is still healing and we can't expect you to remember anything before your mind is ready."

"I know, I just wish I could remember everything in those

letters. Maybe it would make things much easier on us. I can't even remember why I came here and my mother just tells me that I came here looking to be happy when I left."

Jayden smiled and led the way into the kitchen, turning on the lights. "Oh yeah? Any idea on what she wants you to be happy about?"

"Not a clue. She won't say more than all she ever wanted me to be was happy."

"Do you believe her?"

Meilan shrugged as she took a seat at the kitchen island. "How do you believe a person you can't remember ever knowing? I want to believe that my mother wants me to be happy, but then why were all those letters such a secret?"

Jayden sighed as he started pulling out pots and pans. "A lot of things happened. What do you want to know?"

"Why did I move across the country?"

He stiffened as he took food out of the pantry, setting it on the island before her. "That's a loaded question."

"So, you do know the answer."

"Yeah, I do." Jayden started heating a pan before filling another with water. He opened a package of beef, slicing it into thin strips. "It's just not something I'm sure you want the answer to."

"Why wouldn't I?"

"It doesn't paint your mother or your father in the best light." Jayden threw the beef into a bowl and washed down the counter before moving on to a bag of flour and a packet of yeast.

"I want to know," Meilan said, staring at him as he made a dough of some kind. "What are you making?"

Jayden smiled and looked up at her, his hands covered in dough. "Spicy beef bao and scallion pancakes. It was the first meal that you ever gave me. I didn't know what to think of the food when you pulled it out but it was delicious. Chinese food has been some of my favorite ever since."

Meilan laughed and shook her head, grabbing a small cutting board, a knife, and the scallions. "I guess I'll help chop while you tell me about my parents and the move. How small do you want these pieces?"

"Tiny. And fine." Jayden sighed and set the dough aside to rest before starting on the pancake batter. "Well, your father decided that you and I were getting too close so he packed your family up and moved you across the country to get you away from me."

"Why would he do that?" Meilan furrowed her eyebrows, a particularly harsh chop going through the scallions.

"Because I'm black," Jayden said, his voice tight. His knuckles paled on the edge of the counter. Meilan looked at him, a frown on her face.

"I'm sorry," she whispered as she looked away. "What did my mother do about it?"

"Nothing. She kept the letters hidden and agreed to move you across the country."

"Did she regret it?"

Jayden shrugged as he went back to cooking. "I don't know. She says she does. Your mother has always been a very kind and meek woman – apart from the move – so I would like to believe that a part of her sees how wrong she was to avoid standing up to your father. She did apologize when she and I spoke on the phone shortly after your accident."

Meilan stared down at the cutting board and the tiny pieces of scallion, not knowing how to feel. All of this could have been avoided if their lives had gone differently. If her mother had been capable of standing up to her father. If her father hadn't been worried about a black man and an Asian woman falling in love.

There would have never been a plane crash but she and Jayden may also have never ended up finding each other. They could have naturally grown apart even if they had stayed together.

Meilan sat at the island, quizzing Jayden and trying to remember pieces of her life as he spoke. Though he told wonderful stories, none of them seemed to be real.

Finally, the food was set in front of her. The amazing scent wafted up to her, her mouthwatering as she looked at the plate. As soon as Jayden took a seat beside her, Meilan grabbed the chopsticks and dug in.

She closed her eyes, savoring the food. As her eyes closed, she could hear the sound of kids laughing in the cafeteria and the teachers shouting to keep down. She could see that first day in her mind as if it had just happened yesterday.

She remembered the way the scrawny boy had looked across the table at her as she offered him a pink bento box full of bao. He had carefully taken the chopsticks, stumbling with them and trying to pick up the bao. It was clear he had never used them before, the way that he had fumbled, pinching them between his fingers.

It had been funny to watch him struggle at first, and Meilan had giggled while his frustration grew. He glanced up at her, clearly not sure why she was laughing, and said, "It's hard! I'm not sure how to do it correctly!"

"Keep trying," Meilan had giggled, content to watch him struggle for a little bit longer. There was something about watching someone use chopsticks for the first time that was always funny! Maybe just because it was so easy for Meilan to do it herself at that point?

Eventually, Meilan had grabbed one with her fingers, encouraging him to do the same. She had been able to hear the growling of his malnourished stomach.

He had thanked her several times, juices from the spicy beef bao dripping down his chin. She had insisted that he stop thanking her, that he just enjoy the rest of the food. As they had sat in the noisy cafeteria, he ate every bao in the bento box and half of the ones she had brought for herself. She could remember leaving that lunch and promising to bring him more food the next day.

She could remember the look on his face. The way his eyes had lit up like the sun – or maybe like the moon, because his small smile had been soft, and maybe a little bit doubtful. But the doubt had only lasted for a moment, until she promised him that it wasn't a joke, and she wasn't making fun of him. Then it really was like the sun, the way that he looked at her, its flash burning bright across his face.

It was in the last moment before they parted ways for their next class, that he had pulled her in for a tight hug and thanked her one last time. Her heart had been beating rapidly and she knew her cheeks would be turning pink. It was the exact moment she knew that her crush on Jayden had first developed. It was also in that split second, wiping away a speck of juice that he missed before he left, that she knew it was only a matter of time before she fell head over heels for him.

The memory seemed to come out of nowhere, pushing through the fog clinging to her. Meilan had thought remembering things would make her happy. That it would be a relief to get her memories back. But this one brought with it a pain in her chest so strong she had to press a hand over where her heart lay. It came like his smile had that day, a memory so bright it burned through the darkness that had trapped her mind.

In the wake of the clearing fog, there was a rawness; an ache, a desperation to recognize what had happened as the truth. The memories pushed through the ether, one after the other. At once, Meilan was no longer a pastless woman stranded in the middle of the ocean. Rather, she had found her life raft, and it was taking her to shore. But the waves were still rough, and the surf threatened to drown her even now.

Meilan opened her eyes, looking over at Jayden. She could feel the hot tears tracking down her cheeks as he looked over at her.

"I remember everything." The words slipped from her lips almost unbidden. A part of her regretted admitting it; if her memory was back, if those things suddenly living in her brain were true, this would mean the end of everything that had happened since she had woken up in the hospital.

After all, where had the crush she'd had for Jayden led her? Where had that day in the cafeteria led her? Nowhere good. She might be on dry land, but the memories came with the realization that she was about to be unhappy again. And even worse, she had nearly pulled Jayden into the raging ocean waters with her.

The breath left her lungs in a shaky exhalation. She was crying, though she was trying not to. Her eyes burned hot from the tears, and a scratchiness caught at the back of her throat, as if she had swallowed something the wrong way and a cough was threatening to rattle loose. In that moment, her world spun out of control, her life tipping on its axis as the last thirteen years apart came flooding back.

With certainty, she knew that their lives wouldn't be the same again.

It was scary. It was daunting. Meilan should have been thrilled that her memory was back, but she wasn't. She was, perhaps – if it was possible to be such – even more scared now she could remember than when her past was an empty, black hole.

Jayden leapt up from his chair, rushing to wrap her in a hug. He squeezed her tight, not willing to let his Meilan go again. He could feel the hot tears running down his cheeks as he lifted her from her chair and held on. It didn't seem to be real. She had slipped from his fingers once before, what if it happened again?

The hug was a warm comfort, and one that Meilan was greedy enough to take. She curled her arms around his middle and gripped him in return, pulling herself against him. Her forehead pressed hard against the sharpness of his shoulder, and she drew first one breath, then a second.

Slowly, Meilan gained control of her wild, raging emotions. The tears slowed until she was no longer trembling, and her breath came in more steady bursts. His hand soothed the curve of her back. Eventually he let her pull away from him, and smiled at her.

It was the same smile as before; the one that burned as brightly as the sun. Meilan's heart welled with emotion. She knew what she wanted to do. But she also knew what she was supposed to do. What she was expected to do.

And finally – finally – she could remember what she had done in the past.

"That is amazing, Meilan." He pulled away to look down at her. His eyes drifted down to her lips, wondering if it would be so wrong to show her the affection he knew he had. His heart felt full as he shook his head and smiled. "I am so happy that you can remember us."

"I can," she whispered, reaching up to wipe away her own tears. "You are going to have to tell me everything that I have missed these past few years."

"Sure," he said with a laugh as he pulled her into another hug. "If by a few years you mean over a decade."

Meilan laughed, a strangled sob coming from her. It seemed wrong that it had been so long, but that was the truth, wasn't it? She had been gone for over a decade, and she could only imagine how much had changed during that time. How much he had changed; how much this place had changed.

She hugged him back, relishing the second grip even more than the first one. When she spoke, the word was barely more than a shaky, broken-sounding whisper. "Yeah."

"I will tell you everything that you want to know and more. We have so much time ahead of us. How about we finish this dinner that you made for us and then we can talk more?" Jayden suggested, finally pulling back. He reached up, wiping away some of her tears with his thumb. "I'm so glad that you're finally back with me. I knew it would happen if you just gave it enough time."

At least one of them had been certain about it.

"I was starting to think I would never remember anything," admitted Meilan. "I want to talk now. How have you been able to put up with this for weeks on end? I can't imagine how difficult it has been to be around me when I remember nothing."

She ran her hands through her hair, trying to put herself back together piece by piece. Now that she could remember, her previous lack of memory was almost embarrassing. It sat in her chest like frustration, something that had to be gotten past, but – but it seemed an impossible thing to move around.

All this time, unable to remember their history with each other? It must have been unbearable for him.

Jayden laughed and shook his head, still elated that Meilan was back with him. "We can talk about all of that after dinner. Now, sit back down and start eating."

While they ate, Jayden couldn't bring himself to stop staring at Meilan. She was real. She was here. The woman that he loved more than life itself was going to be okay. If Jayden were being honest with himself, he was worried about all of the things that had happened while they were apart. Now that she remembered who she was, were they too different to make this work? Would she still be in love with him?

Jayden was smiling at her, his white teeth shining perfectly as he bit into his own bao. Meilan studied him, noting the way his cheeks were no longer hollow and he didn't look like one strong breeze would blow him away. He wasn't a starving boy anymore. He was a man. A man who didn't look well. His face was paling and his eyelids became droopy.

"Jayden, are you okay?"

He blinked slowly. "I don't know. I don't feel so good."

"I can call the driver and get him to take us to the hospital."

"I don't want to ruin dinner."

Moments later, he was dropping his bao and falling out of his chair to the ground. Meilan screamed, already dropping to her knees beside him.

Chapter Sixteen

Not that long ago, Meilan had been the one in the bed with tubes connected to her and machines beeping. She had been the one laying on her deathbed while Jayden had stayed by her side. Tears slipped down her cheeks as she clutched his hand while the doctors checked his vitals.

He hadn't woken up since he had passed out while eating. Meilan's world had blacked out after that. She knew at some point she had called the ambulance and rode to the hospital with him but where everything else was concerned with that night, she had tunnel vision. All that mattered was if there was something seriously wrong with him or not.

"Is he going to be okay?" Meilan said, her voice wavering as she held Jayden's hand. "Please tell me that he is going to be okay."

The doctor looked at her. "I'm sorry. It seems that he has entered an advanced stage of kidney failure. We don't know too much at this point. We have put your husband on dialysis to help sustain him but it is only a temporary fix."

"What are his options?" Meilan asked, clutching Jayden's hand tighter.

"He will need a kidney transplant. Even that may not work, however, it is his best chance at living."

Meilan looked at her best friend – the love of her life – lying unconscious in the bed. "I'll do it. I'll donate a kidney."

The doctor nodded. "We can run tests and see if your kidney is compatible but the chances are low. You should know that his best chance is a blood relative."

Meilan nodded, tears forming in her eyes. "Alright. We'll run the test and then we will go from there."

When Meilan came back from testing, Jayden was awake and sitting up in bed. His face had seemed to have lost all color. He looked weak in that bed, like he needed her to take care of him. She saw the irony in the complete role reversal.

"What's going on?" Jayden said as she dropped into the recliner beside the bed. "Why are we here? Where were you? Are you okay?"

Meilan laughed, tears in her eyes. "You have got to be kidding me, Jay. You are the one in the hospital connected to wires and machines and yet you are worried about me."

He paused for a moment, looking at her with wide eyes. "You called me Jay."

"Well," Meilan said as she leaned forward. "That's what I've always called you, haven't I?"

He laughed. "You remember."

"I remember everything but that's not important right now. We need to talk about what is happening to you."

"What is happening to me?" Jayden nodded to the machines. "Nobody has been in here to explain any of this yet. I just woke up before you walked in and let me tell you how jarring that was. Of course, I don't need to tell you. We just went through that."

"You passed out in the kitchen. I called the ambulance and after hours of testing, they figured out that you are in a late stage of kidney failure."

Jayden took a deep breath, closing his eyes for a minute and nodding. When he opened his eyes again, they were lined with red. To Meilan's astonishment there was no confusion, just a nod. "That's what I thought it would be. I should have told you sooner. I've had a kidney infection before and I've been seeing the doctors every few weeks. It was only a matter of time before the kidneys had to be removed."

"Shut up. You not telling me something when I couldn't remember who I was is the least of our problems right now." She could feel the lump in her throat as she took a deep breath, trying to steady her rapidly racing heart.

Meilan's eyes watered, tears rolling down her cheeks. Jayden patted the bed, holding the wires out of the way as Meilan climbed up beside him. She nestled into his side, her tears staining the hospital gown that he wore. His arms wrapped around her, holding her tight as he wished that he could make this all better for her.

"I'm not a match," Meilan whispered into his shoulder between sobs. "They tested me and I can't give you a kidney."

"It's okay," Jayden said before kissing the top of her head. His hands drifted up and down her back. "It's okay. Don't cry. We'll figure this out. I promise."

"The doctor said that if we can't find a donor from your family, then you will have to be put on the organ donation list. But they don't know how long that will take. They don't know how much time you have left."

"It's okay, Meilan. We'll make this work. I'll get in contact with my father and if he isn't willing to do anything then I will go on the wait list for spare parts," he said with a laugh.

"It's not funny," Meilan said, punching him lightly in the

shoulder. "I'm sitting here worried about you and you think that it is some big joke."

"I don't think that it's a joke, Meilan. But you can't be sitting here worried about me."

"And why not?"

Jayden sighed and hugged her tighter as she tilted her head back to look at him. "If this had happened a few weeks ago, you wouldn't be here. Why did you even come to New York, Meilan? What could there possibly be here for you after all of this time?"

"If you have to ask that you're stupider than I thought."

He sighed and leaned back against the pillows. "I don't have the energy to argue."

"Well then, stop trying to pick a fight with me and get me to leave. You always do that when we start talking about something that you don't want to talk about."

"Of course, that has to be one of the things that you remember." He looked at her from the corner of his eyes. "It's not that I don't appreciate you being here but seriously Meilan, what are you doing here?"

"You read the letters. You tell me." Meilan got out of the bed and started pacing around the room. "My parents moved us away because they were worried about us becoming too close. They thought that we would have to go through a lot of obstacles being an interracial couple."

"I know," Jayden said. "And I have read those letters but it doesn't tell me what you are doing here now."

"Stop trying to pick a fight with me."

"Stop avoiding the truth," Jayden said, his voice harsh. "Tell me why you came to New York. Tell me what you are doing in this hospital. Because if the only reason you are here is to break my heart again, we've been through that before and I don't feel like going through that again."

"I don't want to do this again, Jay. I don't want to go through the miscommunication and not understanding what is going on in the other person's mind. For once, I want us to be honest with each other so you better listen when I tell you that I am not here to break your heart. Or mine, for that matter. Although, out of the two choices, breaking my own heart seems better."

"What are you talking about?"

"I came to New York to tell you how I felt all of those years ago."

Jayden paused for a moment and looked at her. His heart monitor was beating faster. Meilan wiped the sweat on her palms off on her pants and tried to will the tossing and turning of her stomach to stop. Her cheeks warmed as she looked at her best friend, the only person she had ever seen as good enough.

"I loved you."

His face slipped into an unreadable mask. Meilan watched as his hands clutched the blanket in bunches before releasing it.

"Loved," he said softly. "As in past tense?"

Meilan ran a hand through her hair. "Yes, no, I don't know. It's been a long time, Jay. I know that I still have feelings for you but none of that really matters, does it? You were about to marry someone else. You were about to commit the rest of your life to another woman. It was stupid of me to think that flying here would suddenly dredge up the old feelings. The plane accident was a sign from the universe. I never should have gotten on that plane."

"Do you mean that?" Jayden's voice was hard as he looked at her. "Because if you think that coming here was one big mistake, you better leave this room right now. In fact, go back to the Hamptons, pack up, and leave."

With blurry eyes and an aching heart, Meilan turned away from Jayden. She didn't want him to see her tears. The truth was that she didn't know what she wanted or what she had been thinking when she got on that plane.

You weren't thinking, the little voice inside her said as she walked out of the hospital room. *None of that conversation went the way you wanted it to.*

Maybe things would have been easier if her memory had never come back. At least then she wouldn't know that she had just lost her soulmate for the second time.

She swallowed hard, tears blurring her vision. Meilan was confused about what all of this meant. Though she still loved Jay, was it as simple as falling back together? It couldn't be that easy.

Her head spun with everything that she could have said differently if she wasn't tired and overwhelmed. She would have told him that she still loved him, that she was scared of that love and what it might mean now that he could die. There was a large part of her that was screaming at her to run back inside and fix things.

Instead, she kept walking away from his room. She didn't know what he was feeling. In fact, she didn't know how she was feeling. She wasn't ready to break her own heart yet. Facing the possibility of not being loved in return plus Jay being in the hospital with kidney failure was too much for one day.

"I love you," she whispered as she turned back to look at the hospital.

Chapter Seventeen

Your kidney is not a match.

Over and over the thought played in her mind. A few days had passed since she had seen Jayden. Not once had he called or answered any of her calls. Meilan didn't know what else she could do in New York. Her kidney wasn't a match and the love of her life never wanted to see her again. Not that she blamed Jayden. It had been entirely her fault that their conversation went sideways.

You should have told him how you really feel.

Tell him that you've been miserable without him.

Tell him that you've never loved anybody the way that you love him.

You need to tell him everything that you have always wanted to say.

When it came down to it, there was only one thought stopping Meilan from doing all of the things that her heart was screaming at her to do.

What if he doesn't love me?

It was nearly as heart-wrenching as hearing her kidney

wasn't a match. She could have lived with Jayden hating her for the rest of his life if she had been able to save him. Now, she was nothing more than the girl who had come in with amnesia and broken up his engagement.

"Dad would love that story if he was still alive," Meilan said to herself as she put her last shirt in the little suitcase she had found. "He would gloat. Say that he knew this is how things would turn out this way all along. I doubt he ever would have considered that it would have been my fault though."

Meilan laughed to herself and closed the suitcase. She would leave New York tonight and head back to California.

The room was as she had found it the first night. Meilan sighed and closed her eyes for a minute. She wished that she had remembered Jayden. Maybe their time together would have ended differently. The last thing she had wanted was to sour things between them further.

Meilan took one last look around the house, checking for anything that she could have missed or anything that Jayden might want into the hospital. However, his house in the Hamptons didn't feel like him. There was nothing around that she thought he would have liked. Nothing about football or books, nothing that reminded her anything of him.

When she was on the front porch, her cell phone started ringing. Emma's name flashed across the screen. Meilan cringed. A conversation with the slighted ex-fiancée could only end horribly. Yet, there was something that had her sliding her thumb across the screen.

"Hello?" Meilan said, her voice hesitant as she leaned against the porch railing.

There was a sniffle on the other end of the call. "Hey."

"Are you okay?"

Emma chuckled. "That sounds wrong, doesn't it? The woman my fiancé left me for asking if I'm okay."

"If it makes you feel better, nothing is going on between us and nothing has ever gone on between us."

"It doesn't but thanks for trying. I saw the way you two look at each other. I didn't want to believe it. I didn't think there was anyway that he could still have feelings for you years later. Turns out I was wrong. Anyway, that's not why I'm calling."

"Why are you calling then?"

Emma sighed and there was a long pause on the other end of the line followed by another sniffle. "I made a lot of mistakes with our relationship. I'm not going to let him die though."

"I'm a little confused," Meilan said. "What are you talking about?"

"His father could be a kidney match. I tried getting Kevin looking into his father."

"Why are you telling me this?" Meilan asked. She sighed; she already knew that Jayden's biological father could be a match. That wasn't the issue. The issue was trying to get in contact with him. She doubted that Emma would be able to help her with that. She wasn't sure Jayden would even want her help right now.

"I didn't get anywhere with Kevin. He refused to help me. Maybe he'll help you."

"I don't know how to get in contact with Kevin."

Emma rattled off his address. There was a long pause on the end of the phone. For a moment, Meilan wondered if the other woman had hung up.

"I don't care what happened between you two, hell I don't really care about you. But I do care about him. So, before you tear apart a good man once again, please save his life."

There was no goodbye. Instead, Meilan was left with a dial tone and an uneasy feeling in her stomach. Jayden would never forgive her for inserting herself into his life like this. Still, she found herself getting in the car and driving into the city. It was the least she could do for Jayden after all that he had done for her.

Meilan had hurried to write the address down on a piece of paper which was why she wasn't sure that she had arrived at the right place. Kevin's apartment was located above a tiny Korean barbeque shop down a dark alley. People went in and out of the shop while she climbed the rickety stairs at the side of the building.

Pounding her fist against the door, Meilan waited until the door creaked open. Kevin stared at her, a gun on his hip and his arms crossed over his broad chest.

"What do you want?" he asked.

Meilan rolled her eyes and pushed her way inside. "Answers. A little birdy told me that you will be the one that has them."

Kevin scowled and slammed the door shut. "I don't know who told you that but whatever it is you're after, it's only going to hurt people."

"So, you do know what I want," Meilan said as she leaned against his kitchen counters. Kevin's scowl deepened as he continued to stand by the front door. "Now, how about you give me the phone number for Jayden's father and when he asks how I got it, I will lie?"

A slow smile came across Kevin's face as he moved across the room to open a small drawer in a table. He pulled out a piece of paper and handed it to her. Meilan opened the slip of paper and glanced at the numbers on the paper.

"You're sure that this is his current number?"

"Yes," Kevin said with a firm nod. "I was following him the other week. It's the right number."

Kevin reached into a drawer beside Meilan and pulled out another envelope. He handed it to her. She flipped it over to look at the seal, raising an eyebrow.

"What is this?" she asked.

Kevin shrugged. "If you are going to be with him, I think it's time you have the full story."

Meilan nodded, the envelope at the back of her mind. There were more important things to consider. She would open the envelope later that night, when she was alone and had time to digest whatever could be in there.

"Pleasure doing business with you," Meilan said as she walked to the door and let herself out. As the door closed, she could hear Kevin laughing inside.

Meilan raced down the stairs, eager to get to a quiet place and make a call that could save Jayden's life.

She only hoped that he would forgive her eventually.

Chapter Eighteen

"I called your father," Meilan said as she walked into Jayden's hospital room and sat down in the recliner. She put her purse on the floor and leaned forward. "He'll be on the next plane out here to see if his kidney is a match for yours."

"No." Jayden glared at her. The hollows beneath his eyes were deeper than they had been a few days earlier. "Didn't I tell you not to come back here? And how did you find my father? I never told you a name. Did you go and find Kevin and make him look for him?"

Meilan shrugged and picked at a speck of dirt beneath her nails. After a moment, she looked up at him while reaching into her bag. "If we want to talk about invasions of privacy, we should probably talk about this."

She threw the folder onto the bed. Pictures of her spilled out of the side. High school graduation, university graduation, her sorority, her birthdays. Every major event in her life was contained within a small folder.

"What is this?"

He averted his gaze, looking out of the window at the stormy skies instead of at her. "I don't know."

"Don't you dare lie to me," she said through gritted teeth. "Why do you have all this? Where did you get this?"

"I hired a private investigator shortly after my proposal."

Meilan barked out a short laugh. "After you got engaged you thought you would look me up? Why? To make sure that your life was going better than mine?"

"No."

"To make sure you still hated me for leaving?"

"No!"

Meilan sighed and leaned back in the chair, running a hand through her hair. "Then why did you hire somebody to stalk me, Jayden? Tell me the truth."

"Kevin didn't stalk you. He went down there last summer and collected everything he could find about you."

"Then why did you send him to California to get my mother?"

"You weren't living with her. She wasn't important when I sent him to find you. He didn't bother to include it in the report – if he even knew which I doubt. You were the focus."

"You still haven't told me why."

Jayden grunted and leaned back in the pillows. "I hardly think that is relevant. Instead, call my father and tell him not to come out here. I don't want to know him. I don't want his kidney."

"Shut up," Meilan said. "Just shut up and quit with the act. You want to know him, otherwise you never would have sent your henchman after him. I don't know why you think that admitting that will hurt you."

Jayden scoffed and crossed his arms. "You have no idea what it's like. Growing up I was too white for the black kids and too black for the white ones. I didn't fit in at all and it is his fault. Maybe if he had been around, things would have been different. Or if he hadn't gotten my mother knocked up, I still wouldn't be explaining to officers that I am not breaking into my own home."

Meilan rolled her eyes. "Wrong crowd to try the poor me, people are racist card. Ever been assaulted with egg rolls on the bus home from school? I did. Now, we can keep going with this game all day or you can start talking about why you had me followed."

"Fine," he said, looking back at her. "I wanted to know if I had made the right choice when I asked Emma to marry me."

"And what does looking me up have to do with that?"

"It doesn't matter," Jayden said, his voice turning ice cold. "You made your feelings toward me crystal clear."

Meilan got up and started pacing, running her hand through her long hair before she turned to look at him. "Idiot."

"Excuse me?"

"You heard me. You're an idiot. If you think that my using the past tense is a sign that I have no feelings for you at all then you are the biggest idiot I have ever met. Yes, I regret getting on that plane. I waltzed in and ruined your life."

"Actually, you raced by on a gurney with a doctor straddling you," Jayden said, a sly smile cracking through.

"Shut up."

"I love you."

Meilan stared at him; her eyes wide. "Excuse me?"

"You heard it and that is the only time you are going to hear it if you have no intention of saying it back. I'm just likely going to die and I don't want to do that with regrets."

"You're not dying."

"I'm not taking my father's kidney either. What if he is a drug addict or an alcoholic?"

"You and I both know he isn't. I saw the files, remember? He is a businessman in a big city who gives a ton of money to charity," Meilan said as she gathered the scattered files and place them on the nightstand. "Your father and your mother were only teens when they had you. She was scared. She ran. He didn't follow. I'm not saying it was the right move but I am saying that you need to have a little compassion. You were no treat as a teenager."

"I only got worse after you left."

"Exactly. Give him a chance. In nearly three decades, a lot can change."

Jayden sighed and nodded. "Fine. You win."

"Good," Meilan said. She sat on the edge of the bed and looked down at Jayden. "I got on that plane to tell you that I love you. Instead, I came here and I ripped your life apart at the seams."

"My life wasn't going the way I planned anyway."

Meilan swung her legs onto the bed and leaned back against the pillows beside Jayden. "I still love you. I always have. Every man I meet, I compare against you and none of them measure up. I wrote you all those letters though – the ones my mother never mailed – and I thought that you didn't love me. That you were trying to make a clean break between us."

Jayden chuckled and wrapped an arm around Meilan, pulling her close. "That break was ruinous. It was anything but clean."

Meilan stared at him, her eyes tracing every plane on his face. Her hand came up to cup his cheek. He leaned into it; the stubble rough against her palm. Jayden's eyes closed as she stroked her thumb across his cheek.

"Where does this leave us now?" Meilan whispered as he leaned his forehead against hers. Her eyes flickered down to his mouth for a moment before she met his gaze once more. It was steady and warm, the boy that she had fallen in love with coming forward once more.

"Right where we should be," he said before leaning in to kiss her.

Chapter Nineteen

Meilan and Jayden walked through the park, looking at the flowers. Condensation dripped down Meilan's fingers from the cup of iced coffee she held in her hand. When she and Jayden had been younger, they spent most of their weekends in Central Park or at the zoo. Other times, they would get lost exploring the streets of New York. Sometimes they went to Chinatown and other times they spent their time in Little Italy.

Though Meilan wished that they could do that knew, Jayden was too sick to go far from the hospital. Even convincing the nurse to let her take him to a nearby task was like fighting a war. Meilan had to promise to keep the trip within a certain time limit and as stress-free as possible.

"So," Jayden said with a smirk as he looked down at Meilan. "What are we? Who is moving across the country for who? Where do we go from here? Because I have to tell you, I let you leave once and I'm not about to do it again."

Meilan laughed as he slung his arm across her shoulders. "That's a lot all at once."

"Girlfriend and boyfriend. I'll move. Married."

Stumbling over her own feet, she looked up at him. "What?"

"You heard me. Dating. I'll move across the country. We're getting married."

"Don't you think that is moving a little fast?"

Jayden laughed and shook his head. "No. I've been waiting for you for thirteen years. Getting married seems like a perfectly logical step."

"How about we talk to your father about getting you a kidney first? Then we can talk about marriage."

"We're getting married."

"That's not a proposal."

Jayden frowned. "Take pity on a dying man."

"Idiot."

He leaned close, his breath fanning over her ear. "You love me."

"Yes, I do love you. Either way. We have to meet your father now. Are you ready?"

He sighed. "No. But let's do this."

When Meilan thought of Jayden's father, she hadn't pictured a man who looked exactly like Jayden. She had always supposed that he looked more like his mother than he would have his father. However, when they met Henry, it was as if she was looking at Jayden's twin.

"Hello," Jayden said, looking at his father. "Nice to see you after all these years of abandonment. How have you been? Living an entirely different life, I would think."

Henry rubbed the back of his neck. "There isn't enough time to express how sorry I am. I couldn't believe it when Meilan told me that you were in the hospital. I hadn't heard from your mother since she left me. How is she?"

Jayden flinched. Meilan put a hand on his back, rubbing soothing circles. His shoulders dropped and a defeated look overtook his features.

"She died when I was a baby. Childbirth, actually."

"I'm sorry. I didn't know. She left one day without saying a word. I didn't even know that she was pregnant."

"You didn't?" Jayden thought that his mother would have told Henry at some point or another. How could you not tell someone that you were having a child with them? None of it made sense to him though he supposed it might if he had ever gotten to know his mother.

"If I had known, I don't know if I would have taken you in but I know that I would have at least sent you a birthday card or something. I was dumb. As I got older, I know I would have regretted not knowing you. Even now, I regret not knowing you now that I know about you. I think that I would have taken you in at some point. I would have never wanted you to grow up without either of us."

"I know," Jayden said, and as he said it, he knew it was the truth. Henry wouldn't have taken him right away. What college kid wants a baby? There was a part of Jayden that knew Henry would have come back for him eventually. After all, he was standing here now.

"You had a good family after that, I hope?"

"Nope." Jayden held Meilan closer to him. She could feel the shaking of his hand against her arm. "There was one woman who didn't burn her cigarettes into my back; I suppose that she was better than the rest."

Henry nodded. There was a long silence between the two men before Meilan finally cleared her throat.

"We have to be getting back to the hospital, will you walk with us?" Meilan asked, pinching Jayden's hand to keep him from protesting. Henry saw the gesture, a small smile crossing his face.

"I would like that."

Jayden looked at his father. "This doesn't mean that things are alright between us."

"You and I are far from good," Henry said, looking at his son. "There have been a lot of bridges burned but I would like to try and repair them, if you are willing."

Jayden nodded. "I'd like that."

Chapter Twenty

E ndless tests were run. Every time Meilan turned around, Henry and Jayden were being whisked away for another test. They were dragged from room to room, poked and prodded, all while she sat helplessly in a recliner.

Finally, Jayden came back late at night looking more exhausted than ever. His smile was weak as he looked at Meilan. Her vision was blurry. *Please let his father be a match.*

"Why are you crying?" Jayden asked as the nurses helped him back into bed. "Don't cry Meilan."

"Shut up," Meilan said with a sad smile as she wiped away her tears. "You're not allowed to tell me not to cry when you're dying after we've finally gotten the chance to be together. Not happening."

"I can tell you not to cry all I want." He opened his arms wide. "Come here."

Quickly, Meilan dove into his embrace. Her heart hung heavy in her chest as his arms formed a tight cage around her. She placed her head on his chest and listened to the sound of his heart beat. Though he was dying, the rhythm was still strong. He squeezed her lightly, his lips pressing against her hair.

"Everything is going to be alright," Jayden said, whispering in her ear. "You are going to be just fine without me if anything happens. And if nothing happens, we have a wedding to plan."

Meilan laughed, though it wavered with the lump in her throat. "You still haven't proposed. You can't say that we are getting married. It's not something you just decide."

One of Jayden's arms moved. A small velvet box appeared in front of Meilan. With shaking hands, she took it and lifted the lid. Nestled inside there was a small amber ring on a white gold band. Tiny diamonds surrounded the stone.

"This is beautiful."

"Will you marry me?" Jayden asked, his fingers combing through her hair. "I'd get down on one knee and all of that but I am both a sick and lazy man."

Meilan laughed and wiped away her tears with the back of her hand. "Don't you think that we are moving too fast?"

"We've been loving each other for thirteen years."

"We've been dating for a couple days."

"Just say yes."

"Yes."

He grinned and kissed her. Meilan's heart was soaring as he slid the ring on her finger before kissing her again. She leaned against his chest, holding out her hand and admiring the ring.

"It's beautiful."

"Yes, you are." He kissed her temple. "If I make it through this, we are going to the courthouse and getting married."

"You need to at least give my mother time to fly out here. And some of my friends."

Jayden grinned. "Whatever you want, Meilan. Whatever you want."

"Whatever I want?" Meilan looked up at him with the honey-colored eyes that he adored.

"Whatever you want."

"Don't die."

He chuckled darkly and hugged her tighter. "I wish I could promise that."

The next morning when Meilan woke up, Jayden was sitting up in bed and whispering with a nurse. Meilan sat up and smoothed down her hair, her cheeks turning pink as the nurse winked at her.

"What's going on?" Meilan asked, her voice rough from sleep.

"We have a donor," Jayden said with a grin that threatened to split his face in half. "Henry is a match. He's going to give me a kidney."

Meilan leapt off of the couch and rushed over to pull Jayden into a tight hug. Jayden laughed and kissed her cheeks, feathering kisses over the rest of her face as she laughed.

"You're going to have to take it easy for the next few weeks and there is nothing saying that the kidney will take, but the doctors think that the outcome looks very good," the nurse said with a smile. "That being said, you have an hour before we come prep you for surgery."

Once the nurse was gone, Meilan burst into tears. She laughed and cried as she sat in the bed beside Jayden. *We have a shot at being together,* she thought as she looked at him. Things were going to be alright. He was going to get his kidney and they would get their happily ever after.

"It's happening," Meilan said as she squeezed his hand. "This is the first and last time that you will ever consider dying on me, you got it?"

"Yes ma'am," he said with a grin. Meilan rolled her eyes but she couldn't keep the grin from her face. "No more death scares, I promise."

"Promise that after you get through the surgery and heal. Okay?" Meilan nibbled on her bottom lip. "There could still be things that could go wrong."

"Let's not think about that right now."

"Okay."

There was a knock at the door. Henry stood in the doorway sporting a hospital gown that matched Jayden's. He leaned against the doorframe, his arms crossed over his chest.

"Mind if I interrupt for a few minutes?" he asked, looking at Meilan.

"Not at all," Meilan said. "I could use some breakfast and a shower. I'll be back before you head into surgery. Love you."

Jayden tried to hold onto her hand but Meilan was too fast. She raced out of the room.

Please don't let them kill each other before the surgery.

Chapter Twenty-One

W hen Meilan returned, Jayden was being wheeled down the hall. The nurses stopped the bed as she approached.

"I'm so sorry!" Meilan said as she grabbed his hand. "I tried to get here faster but traffic was insane."

Jayden laughed. "Don't worry. Just give me a kiss, wish me good luck, and tell me that you'll still be waiting for me on the other side."

"I love you. Enjoy your new kidney. I'll see you when you get out."

Tears rolled down her cheeks as she leaned over and kissed Jayden. When she pulled away, the nurses starting pushing the bed again. She watched him roll away down the hall before turning and heading in the opposite direction.

Meilan wiped her tears away and checked the patient names on the door. Soon, she found the one that she was looking for.

"Hello, Meilan, sorry about this morning," Henry said. The nurses prepping him stepped away for a moment. "Can I have a minute, please?"

One of the nurses nodded and they left the room. Meilan took a seat in the chair beside Henry' bed and stared at him. For a few moments, neither of them said nothing. Meilan wasn't sure what she wanted to say to him. There didn't seem to be enough words in the world. What if this man knew all that Jayden had been through while in the system? What if he knew what his absence had done to his son?

"If you hurt him," Meilan said slowly, her fingers lacing together. "If you walk out of his life again, or make him love you and then leave, or turn out to be a horrible person and break his heart, it's not him you need to worry about. It's me. You run and I hunt. You got that?"

Henry struggled to keep the smile off of his face. "Alright, young lady. I can appreciate that. You must really love my son."

"And you don't love him near enough. Giving him a kidney doesn't make you a good father."

"I know that," Henry said with a heavy sigh. "At this point in his life, I don't hope to be a father to him. I just want to get to know him."

Meilan nodded and stood up. "Thank you for saving his life."

"I would want him to save mine."

With a shake of her head, she smiled. "To be quite honest with you, I don't care what you want. I only want my fiancé to make it out of surgery and recover."

It was nearing dinner time when Jayden was finally brought back to the room. He was alert and smiling, though Meilan suspected the pain medication was the reason for his good mood. After giving her stern warnings about not getting in the bed with him, the nurse left the room.

"You threatened my father," Jayden said with a loopy smile as he looked at Meilan. "He told me about it. Said for a tiny woman you are very intimidating. I agreed."

Ronald Hansen

Meilan laughed and took a seat beside his bed, reaching forward to hold his hand. "Well, I'm not about to sit back and watch him hurt you. I thought that he should know that before he decides how to proceed."

"Scary." He smirked at her. "Like a little kitten. All claws but no real power."

Meilan rolled her eyes and kissed the back of his hand. "I'm glad you're okay."

"I want a monkey at our wedding. And a flower man. You know one of the ones who throws flowers from a fanny pack? I want that to walk down the aisle before you."

Meilan's laughter filled the room, her heart swelled with joy. "You are insane. Crazy. Absolutely out of your mind."

"It's the drugs they gave me. Did wonders."

"We can talk about the wedding later, for now get your rest."

Jayden nodded and closed his eyes, nestling himself deeper into the pillows. Meilan looked at Jayden and smiled. It was time that she made a call to her mother.

"Hi, Mom," Meilan said when her mother finally picked up the phone. "How are you?"

"How are you doing? You said you got your memory back but you didn't tell me anything else. What is happening in New York? Are you and that boy together?"

Meilan's hand clenched into a fist at her side. "He is not *that boy*, mother, and you know it. He is Jayden. That's all he has ever been. Maybe I shouldn't have called. I don't know if you're ready to hear what I have to say."

"No," her mother said quickly. "Don't hang up. Please tell me. I'm happy that you're happy. I shouldn't have called him that. Old habits die hard. I will be better, I promise. If you love him and you are happy then I am happy for you."

"Jayden had to have a kidney transplant."

132

"Are you alright? Is he alright? How are you holding up?" Her mother's questions came in rapid-fire Mandarin.

"Mama, it's okay. He got his transplant and he is in recovery now. I'm a little worried and we have to watch for infections, but as long as he gets through the next few weeks, things are looking very good."

"Excellent."

"That's not why I'm calling though." Meilan started to pace from one side of the room to the other. She paused to look out the window at the sun, running one hand through her hair before resuming her pacing.

"Why are you calling me then?"

"Jayden and I are engaged."

The pause on the other end of the line was longer than Meilan would have liked. She waited for minutes, the sound of her mother's breathing the only noise that broke the silence between them.

"Mama, say something."

"Why so soon? Are you pregnant?"

"No!" Meilan pinched the bridge of her nose. "I'm not pregnant. He proposed before he went into surgery. Nothing is saying that we are getting married right away but we will be getting married one day. I want you to be happy for us, mama."

"I am happy for you. So happy. Congratulations, my darling daughter. All I have ever wanted is for you to be happy. Please know that. If I had been a better woman, a stronger woman, I would have never let your father tear you two apart. I wish that I had told you about hiding the letters sooner. If I could go back and change the past, I would."

"Do you mean that?" Meilan asked, a lump in her throat and tears in her eyes.

"Of course, I mean that," her mother said. "I love you, Meilan. I want you to be happy and I want you to experience finding the love of your life. If that man is Jayden, I will be there to walk you down the aisle and do whatever else you need me to do."

They spoke for a few moments longer before the call ended, tears still streaming down Meilan's cheeks. Jayden's bed was rolled into the room and pushed against a wall. He was somewhat alert, a sleepy look still in his eyes as he stared at her.

"Meilan? What's wrong? Why are you crying?"

Meilan shook her head and clasped her hands together behind her head, staring up at the ceiling and trying to breathe. Her breath was coming in short bursts and the room seemed to be closing in around her.

"Meilan, I need you to breathe or else I have to get out of this bed to comfort you and I'm not supposed to do that."

Finally, Meilan looked at him, tears still blurring her vision.

"I called my mother and told her about us."

"Did it go like you thought it would?" he asked.

Meilan shrugged, wiping away the tears. "I don't know how I thought that it would go but it certainly wasn't that way."

"Come here," Jayden said, patting the bed beside him. "Tell me what happened."

"She is happy for us. Very happy. She said that she wanted to be the one to walk me down the aisle and we started talking about wedding plans and starting a family."

"Then why are you crying?"

"I never thought that would be the way that she reacted," Meilan said as she curled into Jayden's side, his arm wrapping around her. "I thought that she would react like my father would have but she didn't. Instead of bringing up all of the challenges that we will face, she was happy."

"That isn't a bad thing," Jayden said with a laugh, leaning over to softly kiss Meilan's forehead.

"I know it isn't but we would have been having a much different conversation if my father were still alive."

"We'll do better with our kids. We'll teach them all of the things that we didn't learn growing up and tell them the truth about the things your parents tried to protect you from."

Meilan pulled back to look up at him. "You really think things will be different with our own family?"

"I know that things will be different. How could they not be?"

Meilan nodded and leaned against the pillows beside him. "I love you."

"I love you too."

Closing her eyes, Meilan allowed her mind to wander. She didn't want to think about her father anymore. Now, she wanted to dream of the future that she and Jayden would have.

Chapter Twenty-Two
Two Years Later

Meilan smoothed down the layers of her dress. On the other side of the doors, she could hear the music playing. Kevin shot her a wink and patted his fanny pack before throwing open the door. Meilan laughed as she caught a glimpse of him dancing down the aisle. He tossed flowers as he went, winking at most of the older men in the room. When the doors shut once more, Meilan was left to her own thoughts.

The wedding was everything that she had hoped it would be and more. After Jayden recovered, they had decided to stay in New York. There was nothing left for Meilan in California anymore. Her future was with Jayden. Everything she had ever wanted was standing in front of her with open arms.

With Jayden came a new family and new friends. People that loved her. People who accepted them as a couple. There was no judgement or snarky comments. Still, Meilan found herself wishing for something more. Wishing for a family that could accept who she loved.

Meilan shook the thoughts from her head while butterflies beat their wings inside her stomach. She clutched the bouquet in her hands and watched as her bridesmaids filed out one by one. With each opening of the door, she could see Jayden shifting his weight from one foot to another. She had to smile at his impatience. They had both waited far too long for this moment.

"Are you ready?"

Meilan looked over her shoulder and smiled. "I think so."

Henry came over to stand at her side, offering his arm. "Let's go get you married to my son."

With a grin, Meilan took his arm. "Thank you for agreeing to walk me down the aisle."

"I know today is bittersweet for you," Henry said as he reached out to move a stray piece of her hair. "Maybe one day your father would have changed his mind. I've had the pleasure of watching you and my son together. There is no love as true as what I have seen between the two of you. You have to live and do what is going to make you happy. Don't let anyone else ever ruin that for you. You deserve to be happy and loved."

Meilan's bottom lip quivered. "You're going to make me cry."

Henry laughed and pulled Meilan into a tight hug. "Only happy tears today."

The music changed as Meilan nodded. "That's our cue."

Henry offered his arm to Meilan once more. She took it, smiling as the doors were opened. Her mother appeared on her other side, linking their arms together with a smile. Tears welled up in Meilan's eyes as she looked at two of the people she loved most in the world. At the other end of the aisle, she could see her future. Everything that she had ever wanted was waiting for her. Jayden had always been waiting for her, just like she had been waiting for him.

If Meilan had known that this is how their story would begin, she would have travelled to New York years earlier. She wouldn't have spent over a decade comparing everyone to the person that she couldn't imagine her life without.

Meilan grinned at Jayden. His smile spread from one side of his face to the other as he gave her a quick wink. When she reached the end of the aisle, Jayden took her hand from Henry and her mother. He helped her up the steps and together they took their places in front of the officiant.

"Hi," Meilan said, a pink tinge on her cheeks.

"Hi," Jayden said, his grin growing. "I love you."

"I love you too."

She handed her bouquet to her maid of honor before reaching out to hold Jayden's hands. The warmth of his skin against hers calmed her, made her forget the crowd around them. The memory of her mother's absence drifted from her mind. It didn't matter if her mother was here and loved them or not. There were dozens of people who wanted to share their special day with them. There was love all around them.

"Here's to forever," Meilan whispered.

Jayden looked at her, his eyes soft as he lifted her hand to his lips and kissed the back of it. "Forever is not nearly long enough."

A single decision to fly across the country had changed her life forever. That plane had brought her back to the man that she loved. They were soulmates; meant to be together against all odds. In that moment, she knew that the plane crash was the best thing that had ever happened to her.